# THE GLASS EYE

# THE GLASS EYE

## YLANDA GALLARDO

Arte Público Press
Houston, Texas

*The Glass Eye* is funded in part by a grant from the National Endowment for the Arts. We are grateful for their support.

*Recovering the past, creating the future*

Arte Público Press
University of Houston
4902 Gulf Fwy, Bldg 19, Rm 100
Houston, Texas 77204-2004

Cover design by Mora Des¡gns

Names: Gallardo, Yolanda, author.
Title: The glass eye / Yolanda Gallardo.
Description: Houston, TX : Arte Público Press, [2019] Identifiers:
  LCCN 2019010957 (print) I LCCN 2019012463 (ebook) I
  ISBN 9781518505645 (epub) I ISBN 9781518505652 (kindle) I
  ISBN 9781518505669 (pdf) I ISBN 9781558858787 (alk. paper)
Subjects: LCSH: Puerto Ricans—Fiction. I GSAFD: Humorous
  fiction.
Classification: LCC PS3607.A41548 (ebook) I LCC
  PS3607.A41548 G57 2019 (print) I DDC 813/.6—dc23
LC record available at https://lccn.loc.gov/2019010957

♾ The paper used in this publication meets the requirements of the American National Standard for Information Sciences—Permanence of Paper for Printed Library Materials, ANSI Z39.48-1984.

19 20 21 22          5 4 3 2 1

*To my sister Joanie's sons, Edward and Christopher Marin, who have brought only joy and happiness to my life.*

# ～ ONE ～

DOÑA AMADA could see more with her one eye than most people could see with two. It was even rumored Amada removed her eye for morning prayer, leaving it to watch over her children as they ate breakfast. The children themselves would not confirm or deny the rumor, it seemed as though they wanted to distance themselves from the mysterious work of their mother. She could see the past and she could see the future. The present was left to the bright, shiny marble that had replaced her other eye, torn from its socket by her husband's jealous mistress. Sarah was her name, and her remains are said to be buried in scattered parts of Westchester County, though this doesn't stop people from seeing her.

Sarah sightings have been reported as far away as New Orleans during Mardi Gras, where an old neighbor saw her throwing beads to the revelers from a balcony. Others saw the ghost of Sarah at George Washington's Headquarters in White Plains, occupying his chair while trying on his very tall boots; at the Westchester Kennel dog show she caused many doggie accidents; at St. Peter and Paul's church where her likeness has been seen in photographs, posing angelically next to the statue of the Madonna. The sighting most gossiped about is the one at Yonkers Raceway, where she was seen running down the stretch in competition with the horses for first place.

Many tales have been woven around the mystery of Sarah's demise, but the one consistent legend is that of Sarah's ghost, having collected all of her essential parts, sighted by drunken commuters on nights when the moon is full. They see her swimming in the river, trying to make her way back to the Bronx.

# ～ Two ～

IN SPITE OF HIS LOOKS AND HIS SIZE SEVEN SHOE, Alberto had a way with the ladies, and he knew it. Perhaps it was his smile and the twinkle in his eye that made them go after him, but go after him they did. He found that the more he ignored them, the more they chased him, and the more his head did swell. His ego became unbearable. His ears already being larger than life, his head grew to a size that matched.

The men in the barrio grumbled at the fact that many times they would have to pay for their delights, while the same were given freely to Alberto, "the limp-wristed *pequeña pinga*," as they began calling him. Having never seen him in the company of another man, they groused at the possibility that there was no truth to the rumor of his homosexuality, forgetting that it was they themselves who labeled him that way from an early age when he refused to play baseball and other sports with them. It was now too late to accept the fact that they had been mistaken. Besides, no real men manicured their fingernails, unless they were movie stars, and everyone knew that all of Hollywood was "like that."

The fact that his father owned a *bodega* didn't hurt his status with the ladies either. They would enter the shop with lascivious smiles, some golden, some toothless and, yes, even some very attractive, hoping to take home an extra chicken cutlet or green banana. The more brazen women would seductively lift oranges or grapefruits to their bee-sting breasts, which were invariably pushed up with rubber falsies or as much tissue paper as their c-cup brassieres could hold. Others hid their lips with the same lace handkerchiefs they would use to cover their heads during Sunday Mass. It was not a randomly chosen action by Father O'Connor, whose eyes searched the red and bleached-blonde heads for lipstick marks, to remind certain ladies they were due for confession. Once there, the same sirens would pound their breasts with regret and later expiate their sins with innumerable Lord's Prayers and Hail Marys.

Collusion with the Devil was murder on many a pair of nylons, but this did not deter them from continuing their mating dances once they left the church, knowing they were cleansed for the moment of any of the previous week's wrongdoing. It wasn't that they were bad girls. It was only their thoughts that they needed to confess. None of them actually did anything, but it was fun to think about it and think they did.

Alberto was not a churchgoer, except on special days when his mother and father went. These, of course, included Easter, when everyone wore hats and new clothes; Palm Sunday, when everyone could be seen carrying bright green palms which would replace last year's faded ones and Ash Wednesday, when no self-respecting Catholic would dare show a forehead in public that did not bear a black smudge. A clean forehead was proof that one did not attend church regularly, and the whispered label "hypocrite" was difficult to endure for an entire year. Children, who felt that money earmarked for the poor was much better spent on egg creams or sugar cane, simply thumbed dirty automobile tires and then their own heads, knowing no one would recognize the difference. Few people did, and some of these children kept up the practice into adulthood, cigarette ashes replacing the tires.

Since these obvious days of worship were few and far between, Alberto had no idea that he was the topic of discussion at many a dinner attended by Father O'Connor and the other parish priests who, no doubt, ended up having to say the Lord's Prayer and Hail Marys also. Instead, Albertico, as the women loved to call him, reveled in his good fortune and made certain that every woman who came into his father's shop was treated to a bright smile and an adorable wink that let each one know she was the special one and not just one of the many.

His father, Don Pepitón, enjoyed his son's popularity, living his life vicariously through him. But what he enjoyed most was the fact that his business had been booming ever since his only child hit puberty. He could not imagine why his son received so much attention from the ladies, but he made sure to thank the Lord every day for having blessed him with such a remarkable son.

Alberto's mother, Doña Antonia, was a different story. Her theory was that all women were *putas*, herself and her mother excluded, and no woman would ever be good enough to bear her son's children, which would no doubt be numerous. She did want grandchildren, fervently, but she cried daily at the fact that there was not another way for them to be conceived. The thought of her little Albertico laying with any woman literally sent her into convulsions. One time, in fact, her seizure was so intense that Don Pepitón had to close the shop after a visit from three not-so-very-tactful ladies. They had come into the shop seemingly to get groceries, but quickly showed their true intentions. Antonia was ready for them. She knew it was not an accident that they damaged as many avocados as they did, feeling for their ripeness, one digging a hole to the deepness of the pit with her purple fingernails while giggling incessantly in the direction of Alberto. It was no accident either that the cleaver flipped through the air from Antonia's hand and barely missed beheading one of the floozies.

With shrieks of fear from the ladies and many *perdón*'s from Don Pepitón, they escaped to the street like chickens from a poultry shop. From then on, they would peer through the windows, making certain Doña Antonia was nowhere in sight before entering the *bodega* to continue parading their wares.

Women would wiggle in, slither in, some even danced in. Don Pepitón, as much as he enjoyed their performances, enjoyed the money he made from them even more.

It was only when Señorita Amada entered the picture on that "Godforsaken day," as Albertico's mother would say, that the *mierda* hit the fan. This was no ordinary young girl. There was definitely something wrong with her, for not once did she glance in Alberto's direction; not that he didn't try to get her attention. He winked and smiled and cleared his throat much too obviously, even went so far as to keep his thumb off of the scale when he weighed her one pound of ground beef, or as she called it, "chopped meat." All of Alberto's posturing was neglected by the lovely young girl who paid for her purchase, eyes lowered, and left without so much as an *adiós*. This display did not go unnoticed by Doña Antonia, who rebuffed her son, calling him an idiot and swearing he would never work in the *bodega* again since he was giving away the food and could no longer be trusted.

That was the day Alberto was banished to work in his uncle Pedro's gas station, where his manicured hands turned black and splintered with steel as they became one with the cars he serviced. To his benefit, he gained freedom from his mother's scrutiny. There was also an old, red Buick that would be his if he could get it running, which he eventually did, much to the surprise of his uncle. He had the same gift with automobiles that he did with the ladies, and that knowledge brought him newfound fame in the neighborhood.

Don Pepitón never questioned his wife's decisions, for they were in reality orders, but he could be heard muttering under his breath at his stupidity for having chosen the wrong Delgado sister for a bride. And Uncle Pedro? Well, he was happy as a clam as his business thrived, as did his imaginary sex life, once his nephew, the "little *maricón,* my ass," came on board.

# ∼ Three ∼

IT WAS COMMON KNOWLEDGE that Doña Esperanza, Amada's mother, was a witch. At least that is what they called anyone who believed in spirits. The need for electricity seemed nonexistent in her home, always aglow with candlelight used in *trabajos* against her enemies. These were not the tall, colorful candles in glass that can be found in most supermarkets nowadays. These were the candles that the Jewish people used during their holidays.

There were those who said she bought her candles wholesale, but anyone who spent time with the woman knew that she stocked up during Chanukah, when the larger grocery store chains sold the Menorah candles two for a dollar, much less than she would have paid during the rest of the year. The Chanukah candles sufficed for everyday hexes and were used in place of the tall, richly colored *botánica*-bought candles reserved for special occasions.

There were neighbors who would swear on their mother's graves that they had seen her on fire escapes and rooftops howling at the moon as she conjured up the demise of many an enemy. Word spread that someone had observed her performing a strange ritual the night before Sarah, Alberto's mistress, disappeared after completing her domestic chores for that rich American couple that lived somewhere in Bronxville or as some called it Fleetwood, the town that only pretended to be Bronxville.

Of course, this was all gossip and speculation, no one who came in contact with Doña Esperanza or her young daughter Amada dared to stay near them past a nod in respect or fear. They would make sure to avoid her gaze at all costs, and scurry away as quickly as possible from what they perceived as imminent danger.

What *was* an indisputable fact was that her second husband, El Bobo, as he was called, had a leaking brain. This had been attributed to one of Doña Esperanza's curses and would eventually be the cause of his demise. The locals would be patient, listening to him tell his incoherent, silly jokes at Clarks, the corner bar, as he treated the neighborhood ne'er-do-wells to a nightly *cerveza* while Doña Esperanza waited for his brain to finally dry out completely. His drinking buddies would ply him with endless questions about his wife, which he was only too delighted to answer in what he thought to be all honesty. "Esperanza's first husband had been a Captain in the Bolivian army. He had sent her away fearing she would be implicated in a coup that was about to take place against the government." That was yesterday. The night before that, he regaled them with the also-true, "I swear to God," tale of Esperanza's former husband, the Venezuelan oil tycoon, who had "abandoned her after siring a son with a wealthy Mexican sculptress." There was also "the lion tamer who traveled with Leonardo's World Renowned Circus, who lost his life in a duel with a midget, who had become hopelessly enamored of Esperanza."

Everyone knew these were fabrications. The truth was, "She had been married to a bullfighter who died after being gored in his private parts just one day after having won two ears and a tail in the bullring." This happened in Spain or Mexico, but that was of no importance. What made them all cringe was the injury to his private parts. They immediately covered their own, with empathy for the poor soul. "Apparently he had celebrated with some little chickadee the night before, and Esperanza got wind of his *faux pas*." "No! He worked in the Peruvian copper mines." "He fought with Generalissimo Franco." "He definitely was one of Hitler's henchmen and narrowly escaped death by pretending to be Jewish and fleeing to South America." All true, as he told it, and no one questioned anything he said for fear it might get back to Esperanza and the next candle she lit would have their name beneath it.

Every night, his buddies listened to his stories, only to repeat them to their eagerly waiting wives, who would in turn repeat them to the Latina yentas in *la marqueta* as they purchased their *bacalao* or *plátanos* or pigs ears, while warning their children, with swipes to their heads, not to steal any beans from the sacks to use as ammunition for their brightly colored plastic pea shooters. The daily chatter pertaining to *la bruja's* life had become ritual, and the neighborhood ladies went at it with a vengeance, but in breathless whispers, lest Esperanza's ears begin to burn. Meanwhile, Esperanza made her daily trip to the *botánica* to buy her special herbs and potions, enjoying the fear and notoriety she supposedly ignored.

## ∼Four∼

"YOUR BROTHER PEDRO is the son of a *burro!*" Doña Antonia's voice could be heard booming throughout the neighborhood. Don Pepitón barely saved his finger while slicing a quarter pound of American cheese for the old woman who had just conveyed the news that Alberto had been seen on Southern Boulevard entering the movie house with none other than Amada, the *bruja*'s daughter.

The domino players, who set up daily near the storefront, were nearly blown from their milk crates by the glass-breaking shrieks of the heavy set shrew, who wailed at the thought of losing her only son to "the family of the witch with a *bobo* for a husband!"

"But what can he do? My brother's not a babysitter, you know," Pepitón said, trying to calm her down.

"I know. It's just that I get so angry when I think of my Albertico with the daughter of a *bruja.* It makes me crazy."

"You know," he said, taking his life into his hands, "if he still worked here, we could keep a closer eye on him, but no, you sent him to work with my brother, and now look what happened."

"My fault? Now it's my fault!" Doña Antonia shrieked, heading toward him with fire in her eyes. "Everything is my fault. The world is my fault the way you think. No, you don't think. You only talk. You talk through your ears and you don't say nothing. *Blah blah blah blah blah.*"

"*Cálmate,* Antonia. You're going to get a stroke."

"A stroke?" she shrieked. "A stroke! Why not tell the world?! Why not let everybody hear you?"

Doña Antonia opened the door and screamed to the domino players. "My husband thinks I'm having a stroke. Do you think I'm having a stroke? Does it look like I'm having a stroke?"

The men jumped up and, in unison, replied, "No, no, Señora. How could he think that?"

"Because he's crazy!" And she slammed the door shut again.

"Pedro should have been buried in Cuba, along with all of your ancestors," she screamed, cursing Castro for his part in Don Pepitón's family having immigrating to the United States. Had Castro not taken power, Pepitón and his entire family, especially his idiot brother, would have remained on that island, and she never would have been so unfortunate as to meet Pepitón, become his wife and bear their beautiful, but not exceptionally bright, son. She was ignorant of the fact that because of his big ears, Alberto had been nicknamed *el conejo* by Pepitón's side of the family. She had never been told that the real reason for little Albertico falling from a tree when he was just a boy was due to the coaxing from one of Pepitón's brothers, who told him that flapping his ears would enable him to fly. Pepitón had used the powerful force of three ice cream sodas to keep his son from spilling the beans.

"How could you have let him go to work for your brother?" Doña Antonia screeched, absolving herself and Albertico of any and all culpability. Had he only remained under her watchful eye, he would never have fallen into this trap the *bruja*'s daughter was setting.

Pepitón's efforts to persuade his wife that going to a movie was a harmless divertissement enjoyed by all young people, fell on deaf—albeit pretty good-sized—ears. Pepitón not only recoiled at his wife's insults but also nimbly ducked the containers of Gold Medal milk whizzing by his head and splattering against the deli case.

Having delivered her cruel message, the old woman smiled as she mouthed the familiar words spoken by Don Pepitón to every customer upon leaving his establishment: "Come again."

The argument had lasted about an hour, just long enough for Pepitón's leg to start hurting as it usually did when they argued. Maybe it was just a coincidence, but it never failed to hurt when she argued with him, or when it was going to rain. The pain brought back the memory of the time he and his brothers had *borrowed* a tractor from the farmer next door when they lived in Florida. Their mischief had turned to tragedy when the tractor fell on its side, crushing Pepito's leg. Back then he was as diminutive as his name, and little Pepito was to forever walk with a hitch in his stride, his leg now serving as a barometer of the weather as well as his relationship with his wife. He had not told his parents about the accident at his brother's urging. His parents would have "killed" the three of them for *borrowing* the tractor in the first place, his father would have removed his heavy leather strap and gone at it with them; Mamá, on the other hand, would have gone back in time, spelling out in detail every difficulty the brothers had caused her from childbirth.

Instead Pepito endured the pain, but ended up in the emergency room, nevertheless, after limping long enough to have it seen by a doctor. Eventually his fractured leg healed, leaving that slight hitch in his stride as a souvenir of childhood mischief and brotherly love. Home from the ER, the brothers received their due strapping, but thankfully not their mother's tirade.

Brought back to reality by a potato to the groin, it was agreed that he would have a chat with his brother Pedro—who of course would never be allowed to darken Doña Antonia's door again—

to see what, if anything, was going on between the two young people. As swiftly as the decision was made, Pepitón set out on his mission, driving his second-hand Jaguar to Pedro's gasoline station.

He would have preferred to speak with his son about the surely benign date with Amada, but that was forbidden by Antonia because it might be construed as prying into his private life and God knows, she would never do that! Instead, Pepitón would be the fish, and he alone would have to come up with a way to get out of the frying pan he had jumped into.

As he drove along Bruckner Boulevard, he wondered what had happened to the beautiful young girl he had married so many years ago. She *was* beautiful then, and always, *always* the lady. What had turned her into this shrew that did nothing but scream all the time? Was it his fault?

Nah. He was a good person. He gave her everything she asked for. He never looked at other women, at least not in front of her. She asked him to stop smoking; he did. As a matter of fact, he was an excellent husband and had no idea why she would think otherwise. If one really thought about it, he was a prize, and any woman would be glad to have him.

He turned the corner and barely missed hitting a *piragua* vendor pushing his yellow cart laden with glass jars of colored syrups across the street. Pepitón yelled out a curse. The vendor cursed back vehemently, but after a few *carajos* and *hijo de putas*, they both continued on their way.

Don Pepitón thought about his brother Che, who was the best-looking of the three of them, and wondered why Antonia had not chosen him for a husband. All of the girls were crazy about Che, yet she chose to spend her life with *him*. *There must be something great about me*, he thought. *I'm not bad looking. I'm a hard worker (but so is she). I'm a good provider. I'm a little sexy. Hell, what does she want? Rudolph Valentino?*

Having finally assuaged his ego and rebuilt his self-respect, Don Pepitón was ready to face his brother. Seeing Alberto at the pumps, Pepitón entertained the idea of getting a fill-up, but thought better of it. He knew that his brother's business practices were not all on the level, especially when it came to buying gasoline from a legitimate distributor. Instead, Pepitón pulled up to the air hose and began to check his tires, all the while searching the area for Pedro, who finally emerged from the men's room.

"Air is only for our customers," Pedro growled in an uncharacteristic way, not yet focusing on his brother after having angrily erased the telephone numbers for the latest, greatest blowjobs from the bathroom walls. Pepitón had rarely visited his service station after the day of the grand opening, when his brother gave away free New York Giants glasses filled with beer to the first one hundred customers. He himself, had emptied two glasses, one for himself and one for Antonia, and had not put so much as a nickel's worth of gas into his tank. He had explained that his automobile, being a foreign make, had trouble adjusting to American gasoline. Pedro had smiled in assent, knowing his brother was "full of shit."

After Pedro realized it was his brother wasting his air, he went up to him and they exchanged hugs and *holas.* Pedro turned and beckoned Pepitón to follow him into the office and away from Alberto, who had waved to his father but was occupied at the time, taking care of a sexy blond *americana* who kept explaining that the sound under her hood was more of a "kling-kling" than a "klunk-klunk." The fact that her description of the problem was accentuated by a cute hip wiggle was a big factor in Alberto's request to have her repeat the sound more than once, just to be certain he understood the problem.

Once in the office, Pepitón admired the old Marilyn Monroe calendar that he had lost to his brother in a friendly game of craps many years ago. Since he was much bigger than Pedro, he had tried to bully him into giving it back, but Pedro held his ground. Marilyn was the only woman he had ever loved other than his wife Gloria, and no man was big enough to take that calendar away from him, not even his large brother. Pedro, who stood five feet tall on tip toes, was a tiger when it came to anything he loved.

When Pepitón finally got around to asking the embarrassing questions about his son and Amada, he was answered with an ignorant shrug and a surprise move, which he was not quick enough to stop. Pedro called out to Alberto to come inside, just as his nephew realized that the difference between "kling-kling" and "klunk-klunk" was a loose ground wire.

Father and son spoke of the weather, Marilyn Monroe, the *bodega* and Antonia, but not once did the name Amada or a movie house on Southern Boulevard ever enter the conversation, which was brief and stilted.

While stopped at a light at Hunts Point, Don Pepitón thought about driving straight to Miami, never to be seen again. Having no other excuse for his sudden visit other than the truth, he instead invited his son to come to dinner on Sunday and bring a date—his choice, of course.

Don Pepitón kept repeating, "Oh my God," as he banged his head against the steering wheel, which he did at every traffic light that stopped his progression home, knowing this pain would be less severe than the punishment that would surely be meted out by his wife for his act of stupidity.

# ～Five～

IT WAS NOT HER KINKY HAIR or her slightly buck-toothed grin that made Sarah ugly. In fact, many of the boys in the barrio found those traits quite desirable. There was something nasty in that smile that seemed to promise just a little more than what was expected of the good girls, who usually hid their silly giggles under the delicate fingers raised over their lips whenever speaking to a member of the opposite sex.

It was not her tweezed eyebrows that arched into a position suggesting she knew something was going on at all times, especially something lurking in the evil little mind of anyone who flirted with her. Nor was it the fact that she chewed gum incessantly, imitating the floozies on the movie screen.

What did make Sarah ugly, at least to other girls, was that she was convinced she was put on this earth as God's gift to mankind, making it impossible for anyone to resist her charms. This confidence made her a powerful magnet, attracting a large circle of would-be suitors. Other young ladies were forced to divvy up the crumbs she left behind, none of which were very attractive, especially after Sarah had tossed them away like the seemingly never-ending wads of her chewed-up bubble gum. But once discarded, part of them always seemed to be stuck under her high heels, never having scraped themselves free.

They would mope at her indifference toward them and weep openly in the arms of their new, not-so-giving girlfriends, who found themselves in the position of having to console their new loves with not-too-kind, not-too-harsh words about Sarah. After all, even a second-hand boyfriend was better than no boyfriend at all. None of them relished the possibility of being labeled a spinster.

Anyway, Sarah gave herself freely, becoming at once every pubescent boy's dream and every virginal girl's nightmare. Under tenement steps, in basements and schoolyard corners Sarah made men out of boys, and boys out of men. Her mother, Doña María, a strict Pentecostal who hated sex almost as much as she hated her fourth husband, was blind to everything except her faith. Every night she could be found at the storefront church, singing to her heart's content about Jesus and salvation while banging on a tambourine.

Doña María had something to say about everybody in the neighborhood. She spent her days staring out her window and listening to everything that was said on the front stoop. When no one was around, she had to be content watching who came in and out of neighborhood buildings, at what times and who they were with. If any one of the kids in the neighborhood got into trouble or even had the misfortune to be hit by a car, she was the first to let the mother know, in a way that said to the woman, "This was your fault." Not everyone was fortunate enough to have a window to the front and not everyone was unemployed and could keep round-the-clock tabs on their children. In her mind, that didn't change things. "Then you shouldn't let your kids go out," she'd say.

When it became known by everyone in the neighborhood —with the exception of Doña María—that Sarah was pregnant, it was her stepfather, Don Julio, who took her to have the secret abortion performed by Dr. Montalvo, a drunkard who specialized in illicit operations. Montalvo had lost his license after misreading his charts and amputating the toes from the wrong foot of one of his diabetic patients. This was just one of many errors he had to his discredit: a kidney here, an appendix there, a few ovaries now and then. But these errors were quickly sewn up to become another doctor's problem later on down the line. The toes of a prominent newspaper editor's wife were not. Once disgraced and unlicensed, he forged a lucrative career performing abortions. If he botched them up, oh well, he botched them up.

The one thing everyone knew was that Dr. Montalvo could not be counted on for secrecy. Sober, he was a man of integrity, the same could not be said for him after a few *traguitos* of rum. So it came as no surprise to the neighbors to see the holy Doña María chasing her naked husband down the street, butcher knife in hand, yelling curses at his mother and his mother's mother and anyone else's mother who had had anything to do with his ever having been born.

There had always been speculation as to who the father of Sarah's aborted child was, but when everyone witnessed a shrieking Doña María chasing Don Julio down the street and howling for the safety of his penis, it confirmed everyone's worst suspicions as to the author of Sarah's pregnancy. *Desnudo en pelotas,* in his birthday suit, Don Julio prayed out loud to the Lord for a police officer to suddenly appear, descend from heaven like an angel and safeguard his member while arresting the knife-wielding wild woman in his pursuit. Of course, most people had previously thought any number of young men could have impregnated Sarah. They clicked their teeth in disgust and were glad to be rid of the pervert. There was an unspoken law in the barrio that you didn't fool around with children, boy or girl, and certainly not your own, or you'd be beaten and run out of town if anyone ever found out about it.

Sarah's popularity waned somewhat after this fiasco. Some of this due, no doubt, to the fact that Doña María insisted on keeping her daughter prisoner in her home for six months. Even her previous suitors felt that a sin had been committed. They were also reticent about her body having once held a fetus; her vagina become more than just an outlet for their penises. Even after she had been freed from her mother's prison, the young men still kept away from Sarah for a time, as if she were a leper. And so she had to be content to hang out on the stoop with the few girls who were not forbidden to speak to her, those whose mothers had lives of their own and could not be bothered airing other people's dirty laundry from window to window as they hung their clean wash out on the backyard clotheslines.

But Sarah, although wounded, was by no means dead. It didn't take long before she was once again chewing her gum, sashaying her merchandise and tempting the boys all over again. She knew too well how to weave her magic, and in no time she was surrounded by a fresh group of lovesick Romeos and despised by the girls who were sorry they had ever befriended her.

It was only Alberto, the grocer-turned-mechanic, who never gave her the time of day, and this drove her crazy. Yes, he returned every buck-toothed smile with the flash of his own teeth, but never once did he ask her out despite the overly aggressive advances she made toward him. What pushed this cat-and-mouse game to a higher degree was his infatuation with Amada, who had been declared Sarah's mortal enemy through no fault of her own.

Not only did Sarah hate the witch's daughter, for her relationship with Alberto, but the witch herself had once caught her in a compromising position under the apartment stairs with one of the neighborhood boys. It was then that Doña Esperanza warned her of the possibility of becoming pregnant, reinforcing that warning with a diatribe on morality. Sarah was convinced that somehow the witch had played a part in her unfortunate pregnancy. On the day the rabbit died, Sarah, who had never once taken responsibility for her own actions, swore she would someday get even with the *bruja* and her goody-two-shoes daughter, even it if killed her.

# ～Six～

DON PEPITÓN WAS IN TAHITI, lying naked in the arms of the lovely young native girl who offered him the fruits she had picked in Gauguin's painting. First, she touched them to her lips and then his. Suddenly he was rudely awakened by his wife, who ordered him to go into the cellar to retrieve the good dishes. He looked at his watch and saw that his hour of lovemaking had lasted only five minutes from the time of his last chore.

"*¡Seguro, Capitán!*" he muttered, ducking the wet dishtowel that sailed past his head. She was not to be played with and he followed her orders to a tee. *Too many orders*, if anyone asked him, but nobody did, and he knew better than to rock his already foundering boat by opening his big mouth again. That his leg was hurting again was well deserved, for it was originated by his own stupidity. The weatherman had predicted sunshine all day, and there was no rain in sight, only thunderclouds around Doña Antonia.

What had caused him to ask his son to bring a girl to dinner, knowing that girl would be Amada, was the loose bearing that rolled around in his head since he had left Pedro's gas station? *Was he suicidal? Had he lost his mind?* What he did know was that life was over for him. He would never again enjoy spending time watching westerns on television without hearing Antonia's voice barking over the gunfire in the background, reminding him of the pain she went through at childbirth, only to have him disregard it with one incomprehensible moment of stupidity. He was doomed and he knew it.

He had laid down a new kitchen carpet the night before and retrieved the bronze peacocks from the closet, which now hung on the wall for good luck. He had washed windows, done two laundries, rooted through the living room drawers until he found the lace cover for the spare roll of toilet paper and replaced the missing tile in the bathroom, which he had meant to do for the past few years but never got around to. He polished the silver, the brass, the chrome, his shoes and anything else in sight that could be polished. All of this because he had been foolish enough to invite his son to bring a girl home for dinner.

He had forgotten just how big his house was, and was now glad that he rented the upstairs apartment to his older brother Che, who could not hear the commotion going on downstairs because, although he once had played the trumpet in a band, was now almost completely deaf. The only word Pepitón had heard his brother utter in the past four years was "¿Qué?" Che's wife, however, was a different story. Carlotta never stopped talking and was called La Cotorra, the parrot, by one and all, but never, never—except during a drunken oversight—to her face. There was more than one wager made regarding whether Che's deafness had really been caused by his music. Some had even gone as far as believing that the old boy was not really deaf at all, but just used this as a defense against Carlotta's incessant chattering.

Carlotta had been dead set against moving into Pepitón and Antonia's house, but she warmed up pretty quickly when she heard the rent would be reasonable enough so that she and Che would be able to buy a place of their own someday. Carlotta had fallen in love when she heard Che play at the Tropicoro in the Bronx, but she hadn't counted on his going deaf within a year of their nuptials. She also hadn't realized that there was not too much money in the trumpet-playing business. She had always wanted a house. It would take longer than she had hoped, but she could wait. Besides, now that Che was deaf, she wasn't sure she wanted to move out to the boondocks where no one could hear her if someone broke in and she screamed. Thus, she resolved to make the best of staying put.

Carlotta was a walking encyclopedia. She could speak on any subject, and only a fool who didn't know better dared challenge anything she said. On the other hand, she did dispute everything said by anyone else. If a vase was blue, it was really aquamarine. If a table was big, it was not as big as the one she had seen in so and so's house. If a movie was good, it was a remake of a much better movie. It was a known fact that one did not even have to speak to elicit such a response from her. Everyone remembered or had been told the story of the unfortunate fellow who, quite by accident, let out a tremendous fart during dinner time, only to be told by La Cotorra that she had heard one louder than any sound that had ever come out of Che's trumpet, to which Che responded, "*¿Qué?*"

Staying put meant having to put up with Doña Antonia's griping, but since Carlotta had the place to herself most of the time, she could blast her music and dance to her heart's content until Antonia returned from the *bodega*, which was usually pretty late in the evening. She also loved to sing, as everyone in the neighborhood unfortunately knew. It wasn't her voice that annoyed the neighbors, it was the way she had of butchering the lyrics until they became her own. Back when Che could hear, he would tell her she had a beautiful voice. He would say anything to get laid. Every so often Antonia would get an unwelcome earful of Carlotta's "song" and bang the ceiling with the broom.

However, there was no music today. This was Pepitón's day to suffer. As he rummaged in the cellar, he was pleased that Antonia had formally invited his brother and sister-in-law for dinner.

There would definitely be no lack of conversation. What did cross his mind more than once, however, was to wonder exactly why his wife was going through so much trouble for, as she called her, "the daughter of a witch." Being a simple man, Pepitón had never been able to understand why Antonia worked so hard at pleasing people she disliked while taking for granted the ones she professed to care about, namely himself.

# ~ SEVEN ~

"WHO'S MINDING THE GARAGE?" were the not so very tactful words Doña Antonia uttered upon opening the door for Pedro and his wife Gloria, who were known gate-crashers, showing up uninvited everywhere, mainly because no one invited them anywhere. Pedro's only answer was to thrust a bottle of Cutty Sark into her hands, followed by the words, "I hope we're not late."

Pedro's gas station must have been thriving, for this was the first time in Antonia's steel-trap memory that the couple had come with anything other than empty hands to go with their empty stomachs. Be that as it may, *they should have called first*, Antonia growled in her mind, *even though they would have been turned down*, which was something they both knew and was precisely why they hadn't called in the first place.

Pepitón came to the rescue of his brother and quickly took their coats and bade them make themselves comfortable. Gloria, who had dyed her hair "eggplant" like most of the women in the Italian area of Yonkers where they now lived, was *persona non grata*, mainly because, to put it delicately, her *caca* didn't stink, and also because of the annoying tendency she had of answering English with Spanish and Spanish with English. It was a constant juggling of bilingual mind and tongue to engage in conversation with the woman.

"I love the color of your hair," Antonia lied, trying to determine what color it actually was.

"*Gracias. Es berenjena.*"

"*Oh*," Antonia replied with a bit of sarcasm. "I didn't know Miss Clairol made dye in the color of eggplant."

"*Seguro que sí. Todas las mujeres en Yonkers usan este color.*"

Antonia, no longer wanting to play, 'you speak Spanish, I speak English,' turned and quickly walked to the kitchen.

The men got down to telling old jokes and war stories of their childhood, while Gloria offered to help Antonia in the kitchen by sitting on her skinny behind and doing nothing. When Antonia had slammed enough pots down, making it evident that she was not very pleased with all of the work she had to do, Gloria offered to make the salad, but was quickly turned down because Gloria insisted on filling it with too many carrot shavings, which always overwhelmed the rest of the produce. Many after dinner conversations had been spent discussing her suspected relationship to Bugs Bunny. Instead, Antonia put her to work setting the table, with a strict caveat to be careful not to drop any of the good china. She had never taken responsibility for having previously chipped one of the gilt edges, rendering that plate useless from that day on. Everyone had seen her accidentally crack it against the faucet the last time she had ever been allowed to wash dishes in the house.

Ever the critic, Gloria's teeth clicked whenever she supposedly saw spots on the glasses, and she could barely conceal her alarm that there were no napkin rings. She raised the same alarm every time she set the table and had to figure out how to fold the napkins to make them presentable. "Perhaps fan-shaped? No! Perhaps…"

*Bang*, went the lid on the frying pan, causing the old warriors to jump from their seats. Gloria was escorted back into the living room and told to find some music to put on the Victrola. In reality it was simply a stereo, but to Antonia, who had barely dipped her toes into the twentieth century, anything that played records would always be a Victrola.

Gloria never liked choosing which record to play because she always chose wrong, as they would all remind her. Her taste in music left much to be desired, but it wasn't her fault. How do you choose from a selection that could have belonged to your grandmother? There was nothing up-to-date. There was nothing American. They were all scratchy LPs recorded by musicians who had died years before she was born. But distasteful as this job was to her, it was still better than sitting in the kitchen with Antonia, watching her bang the pots around like a lunatic.

It wasn't long before Che arrived with Carlotta, who was dressed to the nines in "just a little something she had picked up at Lord & Taylor's." Che, on the other hand, sported his favorite flannel shirt which hung over his faded chinos that seemed to perpetually need zipping up. Carlotta had paced back and forth in the upstairs apartment, waiting to hear some signs of life other than the usual shouting, because it wasn't proper to be the first ones to arrive, notwithstanding the fact that she loathed being put to work in someone else's house.

Antonia, having heard the doorbell ring, waited a few moments, thinking Albertico had arrived, and then twirled into the living room, to everyone's astonishment. Having realized her mistake, she quickly recovered and said her hellos to Che and Carlotta, as if they were old friends that she hadn't seen in years.

After exchanging hugs and kisses and looking at photographs of Gloria's new Chiweenie, Pepitón made the mistake of asking the dog's name.

"I named him after my husband, of course."

"You named your dog Pedro?" asked Pepitón.

"Don't be silly," replied Gloria. *"Lo llamé Valentino*, Pedro's real name."

"Since when is Pedro Valentino?" Carlotta chimed in, this being the first time she had heard of it.

"Since their mother named them all after popes," Antonia joined in. "Why would anyone in their right mind name their children after popes? How would you like living with this one here named Innocent?"

"Better than living with Hilarius."

"Who's Hilarius?"

"He is," said Carlotta, pointing to Che.

"That's enough making fun of our mother," Pepitón admonished.

Che said, *"¿Qué?"*

And with that, they were silent again.

Antonia, not wishing to make the same twirling *faux pas* as before, seated herself by the window to wait for her son. He was taking much too long, and she knew in her heart something had happened to him. She was certain they would be getting a call any minute now, telling her the bad news. She was sure her life would be ending in seconds.

Meanwhile, the others, not having the slightest idea of what was on Antonia's mind, munched on *hors d'oeuvres:* spiced ham on Ritz crackers with an olive on top and deviled-eggs that had just a sprinkling too much of paprika. They were not to touch the tuna fish in the celery boats because they were Albertico's favorite. Antonia's grave warning for Pepitón was that he was not to make a drunken fool of himself before the other guests arrived. Why she referred to her son as a guest in his own home was a puzzlement to Pepitón, who opted for ignorance rather than pose the question.

When the old, red Buick finally pulled into the driveway, Antonia quickly deserted her window seat and ran into the kitchen, to check on the *pernil* in the oven and to repeat the grand entrance she had performed earlier. She was not a happy camper when Alberto and Amada entered through the back door and sent her choking on a piece of *chicharrón*.

After a few slaps on the back and a glass of water, they were able to exchange greetings, and in a short time dinner was served. *The quicker the better*, Antonia thought, while indirectly admonishing her son for his tardiness by stating that the *pernil* looked like a "ball of charcoal." Everyone ate heartily, agreeing they had never tasted anything quite so delicious. Gloria gave the ultimate compliment by asking what the secret was to Antonia's *mofongo*. And the *funche*, "Oh my God, it is *divino*."

It was only when it came time for dessert that a lull came over the table. Antonia had made little flan dishes, but decided that it would be rude not to serve the cake that Amada's mother had baked for them. The men had no qualms about taking a slice, despite the silly superstitions of their wives about eating anything touched by a witch. Alberto, sensing the embarrassing spectacle that was about to take place, quickly cut himself a large portion and proceeded to eat it with relish, at which time Antonia, shocked by her son's suicidal move, fainted.

It was a short faint, with a quick revival, but the point was made. No one else touched the cake, and in an effort to be discreet, no one ate the flan either.

After dinner, the men, having stuffed themselves to the gills, retired to the living room, while the women cleared the table and helped with the dishes, with the exception of Gloria, who was made to sit down and dry the silverware, her second most-hated chore.

# ~Eight~

ALBERTO STARED INTO THE EYES OF CHRIST in Doña Esperanza's living room as he waited for the cup of coffee Amada had promised him. The plaster statue positioned in the center of the homemade altar was so lifelike that Alberto could almost swear it was crying real tears. He had tried to divert his attention from the altar by looking at the other objects in the room: the large portrait of Simón Bolívar, who appeared to be looking down on him with just a bit of disdain, a community of diverse figurines on the mantel and the African doll on top of the television set that eerily slumped into a laying-down position when it met his gaze. Perhaps it was his imagination or, as he preferred to believe, the breeze from the open window. Whatever the reason, it did not make him feel very comfortable and it gave him goosebumps. The whole scene was disquieting to say the least.

As Alberto concentrated on the lace curtains, he could not help but wonder what his mother would say if she knew where he was. She had warned him to never darken the witch's door, no matter the reason. If the place was on fire, he was not to step foot in that house. *You never know what can happen to you once you're inside.* Now, for a simple cup of coffee and the charms of the beautiful Amada, he was doomed.

It wasn't that he really believed all of the stories he had heard about the witch. In this neighborhood stories spread like wildfires.

There was the story about the woman with the twitch, where everyone said never to look her in the eye or the twitch would be transferred to you. There was that tale about a man named Ignacio who had laughed at the color of an old man's pants—a male witch unbeknownst to him—only to find himself running home without clothes on, his pants magically disappearing along with his ability to ever    laugh again. There were so many stories and legends, proverbs and taboos that he could only imagine what he'd have to face at home once Doña Antonia found out about his visit to the home of the renowned *bruja*. He tried thinking of any way to keep her from finding out, but he knew somehow she would. She knew everything, even before it happened, and she would waste no time before screaming about it so loud that the whole neighborhood would echo her complaints.

Amada had been sidetracked into the bathroom by her mother, who quickly sprinkled water all around her to ward off any evil thoughts and spirits she might have brought back with her from Alberto's family, especially from that "crazy mother of his. Deep down, wasn't there was something strange about her?" In any case, there was no such thing as being too cautious. Amada, who had been through this ritual daily for all of her young life, suppressed the ticklish giggles coming on, knowing all too well that in Esperanza's eyes, there was nothing funny about the *pasos* she gave.

There were times when Amada hated the fact that her mother practiced spiritualism, but she knew it was a gift that was not to be ignored. *If* you ignored it, you would live a miserable life. Forever. She still would have loved for Doña Esperanza to be like other mothers, who were ignorant of their children's behavior and had to find out about them through neighbors or worse. Her mother knew exactly what she was doing at all times, thanks to her clairvoyant abilities.

Amada had never really had the opportunity to be bad even if she had wanted to. Only once did she lie to her mother—about being in the library when she had been over at her friend's house. Esperanza had just smiled at her, and Amada had blurted out the truth as if she would have lost her tongue if she hadn't, confirming Esperanza's mystical powers.

When El Bobo, who Alberto eventually found out was really named Joaquín, entered the room and challenged him to a game of checkers, he was more than willing to comply. It was as good a distraction as any. Besides, he was pretty good at checkers and, although he didn't want to take the poor old guy's money, he could not insult him by refusing to make a little wager on the game. Alberto had no idea that El Bobo had once been the best checker player in his hometown, and Alberto found himself quickly relieved of the burdensome weight that had once filled his wallet.

When the coffee was *finally* served, Alberto's charm quickly shone. Being an avid reader, he was a wonderful storyteller, which was unusual for someone his age. He would dive into the books he read and find himself rewriting them to fit his imagination, which was endless. He refused to be sad, so when he told the story of *The Lady of the Camelias*, or any other tragic book he read, he would give it a happy ending, enchanting those around him who knew the story but liked his ending better. He told stories of pirates and truckers that no one in his right mind could believe, and yet they were told with just the right amount of believability to make people doubt what they knew to be true. Anyone who thought of questioning a story would find himself in the middle of another story, which would go on until the white flag of surrender could be raised. In this way they learned to sit back and enjoy the stories with everybody else. El Bobo found himself having a difficult time getting a word in edgewise, not that he didn't keep trying. He interrupted with stories that everyone had heard a thousand times already and was finally told to be quiet if he didn't have something new to say. Much to their surprise, he was able to dig deep into his thwarted memory and come up with a few doozies, like the one about the time he climbed a utility pole to help put up a clothesline for his neighbor, only to split his Sunday pants in the process; he did not leave his high perch until darkness because he had not been wearing under-wear and his *culito* was showing. And better still, when he was an altar boy, he replaced Father Donnelly's wine with vinegar, causing a coughing fit and an interruption of the Mass due to an acute case of diarrhea. After that, he was forbidden from entering the church for all time, and not even confession could save him from the devil he had befriended.

Even so, he was no match for Alberto, whose soul still retained all of the joys of life, evoking the colors and tastes and aromas of every episode he retold. Before long, any tensions that may have lingered among the foursome were quickly tossed out the window, as they all laughed together, including Doña Esper-anza, who shocked everyone by saying she was quite happy to have been mistaken about Alberto being a *fairy*, to which he replied that he was just as happy to know she was not really a *witch*. After the longest moment of silence in history, they both burst into laughter. They became the best of friends, or at least for the time being.

When the hour came for Alberto's departure, they all agreed that he should not be a stranger. Doña Esperanza nudged Joaquín and whispered in his ear that they should let the youngsters have a minute alone to say good-bye, *after* he returned the money he had "*stolen*" from Alberto playing checkers.

It had been a great evening for Amada, and for a short while she allowed herself to dream of a happier life. But she quickly shrugged the dreams away as wishful thinking. The following morning, when she went into the kitchen to enjoy one of the cookies she had brought from Alberto's house, she was not sur-prised that the entire bag had been tossed into the garbage can, "Just in case."

# ~ NINE ~

DOÑA ANTONIA LOST HER MEMORY for three days when Alberto declared he was in love with Amada. It was a Sunday. They were preparing for church when he broke the news that he was continuing to see Amada and that she just might be the girl he would want to live with for the rest of his life. Pepitón waited a full minute for the explosion, but nothing happened. Antonia carried on as if she were deaf.

Alberto, seeing an opening, began to extol Amada's wonderful virtues, while Pepitón, not believing his own eyes or ears, just stared at his wife, who remained calm as she served the coffee not even spilling a drop.

"Do you want toast with your eggs?" she asked Pepitón, as if nothing had been said.

"I always have toast, you know that," he replied, looking at her strangely.

"How would I know that?" she shot back. "I'm not a mind reader. And you?" She turned to Alberto. "You want toast too?"

Her sudden amnesia perplexed Pepitón, but he chalked it up to her not wanting to believe what she just had heard. It was when they got in the car and she asked, "Where are we going?" that he said to himself, "Enough is enough." He was tired of the game she was playing.

"Church," he said, gruffly, and drove away.

During Mass he looked on as she seemed to forget when to stand, when to kneel, when to sit. It was obviously confusing to her, and she became agitated. To avoid embarrassment, he quickly walked her out of church before the service was over.

"What's the matter with you?" he asked.

At that, she began to cry.

In all of the years they had been married, he had never seen her cry, and he began to cry too. They both got in the car and drove home in a teary silence.

The three days that followed were hell for Pepitón, with Antonia going in and out of clarity, but things got back to normal and all was good again. He made it a point to speak with Alberto though, and beseeched him not mention Amada to his mother for the time being.

After all, "What she doesn't know, won't hurt her."

"But make no mistake: I'm going to marry Amada."

He and Pepitón agreed it would be their secret for the time being.

Life had become normal again, and all went on as it had before. The store was doing well, Alberto continued to work at Pedro's garage and Sunday dinners continued with Carlotta and Che (Pedro and Gloria included).

# ～Ten～

THE DAY ALBERTO PROPOSED TO AMADA was the day Doña Antonia literally began to lose her senses. Her sense of taste was the first to go in what Pepitón eventually called her *senseless* disease. Day after day, dinner became a curious adventure of the palate for family and guests at their dinner table. An excess of salt and pepper had become the norm, as well as a heavy dose of paprika or cumin on everything white. White had become Antonia's enemy, and any white-looking food was immediately doused with the most colorful spice she could find. Everyone understood that Alka Seltzer was indispensable immediately after dinner, or even in the middle of the repast during a quick trip to the bathroom. Antonia, for her part, found every morsel delicious and would be reduced to tears whenever anyone questioned what they were eating.

The loss of her sense of smell followed shortly afterward, this time to no one's real amazement.

It was not long before Pepitón and Alberto found themselves taking turns in the kitchen, making certain that the roast, or *pernil*, that was in the oven was not charred beyond recognition. Even Carlotta was put on sentry duty; for, as Pepitón reminded her, if his house burned down, she, living in the upstairs apartment, would also lose everything.

Antonia's eyesight was failing. She went to the eye doctor at Pepitón's insistence, but was told she did not need reading glasses. Nevertheless, it became a familiar sight to see her reading *El Diario* with the help of the magnifying glass she had saved from Alberto's stamp-collecting days.

"She's just being dramatic," was her son's view of this ill-defined sickness, but Pepitón was upset that his wife was having trouble with the prices at the *bodega*. It was only when he realized that her mistakes were never in favor of the customers that he thought his son might be right.

It was a short time after she lost her hearing that Pepitón stopped communicating with her, for after one *"¿Qué?"* too many, between Che and Antonia, Pepitón turned into what she described as "a raving mad lunatic," who promised to cut out both of their tongues if he ever heard the word *qué* again. In an effort to keep the peace, and their tongues, silence seemed the best option.

After the initial shock of Antonia's losses, everyone resigned themselves to the fact that these were symptoms of hysteria that would be regained once the fateful words, "I do," were exchanged. And this was precisely what happened. For, as the bride and groom filed out of the church after taking their vows, Doña Antonia declared in a loud voice that "the organist was off key!"

# ~ Eleven ~

IT COULD HAVE BEEN A WEDDING OR A FUNERAL. The same group of relatives who had wept at José Antonio's wake, held at Walter B. Cooke Funeral Home in what seemed many years ago, entered the great ballroom. Some wore the same suits they had worn, or, it should be said, the only suits they owned, ready to party. Distant relatives screeched in recognition, just as they had done at José's passing (only not so somberly), upon meeting others in the family they hardly recognized now that they had grown fatter or grayer or younger or balder. The relatives' newly dry-cleaned suit pockets and heavily beaded bags held the obligatory envelopes containing no more than the very well calculated cost of the food—not counting the drinks—they would consume on that memorable evening.

The mothers of the bride and groom managed to avoid each other, sitting on opposite sides of the ballroom. However, they watched the festivities like hawks, especially Doña Esperanza, who took mental notes of everything that went on. She took an immediate dislike to Sarah and wondered where she had come from. Was she related to Antonia or Pepitón? She remembered having seen her somewhere, but *just* where escaped her.

There was Pedro and Cucho and Quique and Papo and Lupe and Tita and Ding Ding and his brother Ding Dong, who had been so handsome when he was young and now had grown fat and bald and looked very much like a bowling ball. Also in attendance was Fina and None and Nena and Chicha and Caco, who kept asking to dance and kept being declined because he looked like he was having a heart attack when he did dance. There was Mecha and Lalo and Cariplato and Pina, and a host of others who had the misfortune of having been nicknamed at an early age by a doting aunt or grandmother. They were names that, once uttered, stuck for life like the flypaper hanging from kitchen fixtures.

Intermingling with the guests were the not-so-familiar faces. There was Armando, the neighborhood drunk who managed to crash every celebration in the South Bronx by following the Valencia Bakery truck to its destination. Hortensia, who insisted on climbing onto the stage to shake tits and maracas while singing every *bolero* with the band—whose members, at the request of Pepitón, all wore pale-blue satin jackets with dark blue collars over their ruffled yellow shirts. Their attire reminded Antonia of when she used to go dancing and enjoy herself, something she would not be caught dead doing anymore.

Then there was Sarah, who hours before had sat glumly in the back of St. Athanasius Church as Alberto and Amada took their wedding vows. She congratulated them afterward, and led in the rice-throwing upon the couple's departure. Now she stood arm in arm with Coco, the man with the twitch in his eye who was also missing his front teeth. Coco's place in the family tree was a bit shaky because of the bitter fruit it bore.

It took very little time for Sarah to ingratiate herself with the rest of the guests and, before long, she was like one of the family. Her hips swayed beneath a red dress, which seemed painted onto her body as she danced the rumba and the samba and even managed a merengue with El Bobo—or half a merengue, for Doña Esperanza quickly cut in with clenched teeth, leaving Sarah to dance with one of the young boys who could not have been more than fourteen, but who dreamed about that dance for many years afterward.

There were many *oohs* and *ahs* when the bride and groom made their grand entrance into the ballroom, and Sarah managed a smile with her bucked teeth as she dug her fingernails into the thick shoulder pads of Coco's gray suit. Having caught Alberto's eye, she smiled and turned away.

There was the collective groan when Hilda caught the bouquet, as she seemed to do at all weddings, because everyone knew she was gay and had no intention of ever getting married. Many argued that she should sit this one out and let someone else have a chance at becoming the next bride, but Hilda would have no part of that logic, knowing that she was just as eligible as the others, and she dove in like a linebacker for the ultimate prize.

Hilda managed a sexy smile during the humiliating spectacle of the garter wriggling up her leg in the hands of the twitching, toothless Coco, who had caught it happily. The none-too-happy wives covered the eyes of their lascivious mates and clucked their disapproval.

All in all the evening seemed to go well, with only occasional grousing about who should have been seated at whose table, who had a little too much to drink, who was flirting with whose wife and who had stolen the bottle from whose table. There was the interruption of the mambos and *boleros* for the obligatory line-up for the *pasodoble*, which seemed to occur every half hour and which very few people, with the exception of the older ones, knew how to dance.

The photographer from Austin Studios appeared to be everywhere, taking the conventional photos of the bride and groom alone, the bride and groom with the bride's family, the bride and groom with the groom's family, the bride and groom with both families, the bride and groom with the best man and the maid of honor, the bride and groom sipping champagne, the bride and groom cutting the Valencia cake and, of course, the bride and groom feeding each other the cake, making certain they mashed some of it on each other's faces.

Throughout the festivities, Doña Antonia remained seated at her table, crying in her one Piña Colada too many as she managed to find fault with everything. The potato salad was too salty, the cake was too dry, the music was too noisy, the ballroom was too small, the guests were too loud. It all added up to the miserable fact that she was losing her son.

Don Pepitón had tried earlier to assure her that everything would be all right. He pointed out the fact that they could see the Hudson River from where they sat and it was sparkling in its beauty, which only reminded Antonia of how many people had drowned in it. When he spoke of the Palisades, "so beautiful," he once again was rebuffed by: "Big rocks, that's all they are. We're lucky they don't tumble down and kill all of us."

"You've lost all of the poetry in you," he told her, having grown tired of listening to her carping.

Pepitón got up and joined a group of men who exchanged nudges as they spoke of the impending honeymoon, or what they collectively found humor in calling "Opening Night."

Doña Antonia, for her part, welcomed the attention she received from the stranger in the bright red dress, who she assumed was related in some way to Amada. After all, everyone else in *her* family had deserted her, and here was a young girl, wise beyond her years, listening intently and with such understanding to a mother's pain.

Doña Antonia began her story with the difficulty of childbirth and continued on to the present. She managed to stop time with every line, as if it had happened yesterday; his first communion, his schooling, his every birthday, from the first to the last. The first time he stood up. The first time he fell down. When he was potty-trained and when he took his first steps. No one had been there to help her because, of course, Pepitón had been too busy and, besides, it was *her* story, not his. Everything had been so hard for her, and now someone was listening and finally cared.

Doña Esperanza, on the other hand, had assumed Sarah was somehow related to Alberto, and had instantly disliked her. There was something familiar about that girl, although she could not put her finger on it. She had long since forgotten their run-in under the stairs. Sarah had acted friendly enough, but it was that saccharine smile of hers that had left a bitter taste, and Esperanza did not like it at all. Her eye zeroed in on that red dress like a scope on a sniper's rifle, and she was prepared to shoot at any given moment. But Sarah, growing wiser by the day, kept her distance from the old *bruja* throughout the evening. When the newlyweds finally said their goodbyes, it came as no surprise to Esperanza that the girl in the red dress was nowhere to be seen. She made a mental note to speak to her spirits about it the next morning.

～ ～ ～

And speak she did. She tried and tried to figure out what had bothered her so much about this girl, but nothing came. She called upon her spiritual guide to help her, but to no avail. It was as if someone was blocking her every thought and there was nothing she could say or do to break through this barrier. There was so much confusion in her thoughts, and each time she pondered the issue her head would hurt and she had to lie down. Whatever it was, it was stronger than she was, and it was evil.

## ~ TWELVE ~

WHEN CARLOTTA AND CHE were given their eviction notice, La Cotorra's squawks could be heard as far away as New Jersey. Carlotta had forgotten that they had rented the apartment upstairs with the understanding that once Alberto got married they would have to leave. The apartment would then belong to the newlyweds. That agreement had been made more than ten years earlier, when Alberto was just a child, and it was never mentioned again. Until now. Besides, his effeminate nature had precluded that possibility, and Carlotta had settled in for what she thought was life.

Screeching about the loss of the neighborhood friends she had made, she was coldly reminded by Antonia that she rarely left the house except for work or shopping, and she really had no friends to speak of. One could not possibly count strangers, who only nodded to her in passing, as friends. When she complained of the high cost of renting a new apartment she was reminded by Pepitón that she hadn't paid rent in quite some time and therefore must have a huge nest-egg stashed away. This news of Carlotta and Che's freeloading came as a shock to Antonia and only served to further exacerbate the unpleasant situation. Had she been aware of her rent-free guests, she would have thrown the deadbeats out long ago and put an end to the free Sunday dinners.

Argument after argument was pursued, only to be dismissed as ridiculous. Carlotta could work as a manicurist almost anywhere and did not have to depend on her position at The Velvet Twist beauty salon, which was only a subway ride away. There were schools in every neighborhood, not just the one a few blocks away in which she had planned to enroll her own children someday, if she ever had children—which they all knew was impossible, unless there was a miracle in the medical field and hysterectomies became reversible. Carlotta's last ditch effort was her husband's loss of hearing, but that was quickly rebuffed by Antonia with "What in God's name does Che's deafness have to do with anything? He could just as easily not hear in another neighbourhood."

After a great deal of shouting it was revealed that Pepitón and Pedro had looked at an apartment in Pedro's building in Yonkers.

"Yonkers? Why would I want to live in Yonkers?" Carlotta screamed.

"Because that's where Pedro and Gloria live. You love their apartment. You're always telling them how lucky they are to live where there are trees. *And* they have a terrace."

Carlotta was listening now. "Will I have a terrace too?" she asked.

"But of course. And if I remember correctly, the apartment that would be yours is even bigger than Gloria's," Pepitón said, attempting to sell her. "The closet space puts the one upstairs to shame, just right for all your beautiful clothes and everything. And this way you would still be living close to relatives, only a short train ride away from the Bronx."

They almost had her convinced until Antonia balked at the promise of helping them with the security money. She was quickly reminded by Pepitón, under his breath, that it was the only way they would ever get them to move out.

Although La Cotorra was not entirely thrilled with the situation, she realized she had very few alternatives, for after inciting Che to take a stand, "like a man," his response remained, "*¿Qué?*"

What had seemed a total disaster to Carlotta soon turned into a not-so-bad situation after learning that she had much more in common with Gloria than she ever had with Antonia. They both loved to shop, they both loved to go dancing but, more important-ly, they both disliked Antonia. Not that she was a mean person, they would agree, but she wasn't the sweetest woman on earth either. "You can say that again!" What really irked them was the fact that they each had a mother and did not need another one to remind them of their faults, especially one who had quite a few shortcomings of her own. And Antonia *did* have her faults, they would remind each other over coffee every day for the rest of their natural lives, or until they no longer deemed each other best of friends.

They would carp about Antonia's inability to have fun, her lack of taste, her brutal tongue, her lousy cooking, her unnatural doting on her son but never once did they mention her biggest flaw, which was that she had more money than they did. They were just jealous more than anything.

"If I had the kind of money they have, I'd be living in the Hamptons with all of the rich people instead of the Bronx like they do," Gloria would often say.

Carlotta would agree with her. "And they're both very cheap. You'd think, with them owning a *bodega,* they would at least let us get our groceries at half price. But no. We have to pay the same as everybody else, as if we were complete strangers."

This was a lie, of course, but the discount each of them received was not enough to satisfy them. They were family and not the public; they expected to get everything for free, never tak-ing into account that it cost Pepitón and Antonia money to buy it all in the first place.

Carlotta also relished the fact that she could play her stereo without the accompaniment of a broom banging on the ceiling beneath her feet. And the bosom buddies could now accompany each other to the Palladium on Friday nights. Everyone knew the Palladium was the place to go.

Che refused to set foot in a nightclub and Pedro was always working or much too tired to go dancing, so, other than an occasional grumble now and then, the men acquiesced to their wandering wives who, as they were constantly reminded in case they had forgotten, "were not prisoners."

Their trips to the Palladium were harmless enough because, as amazing as it may sound, they really did just go there to dance. The music was wonderful and the dance floor crowded, especially when Tito Rodríguez or Tito Puente or Vicentico Valdés were on stage. Everyone who was anyone went there, even Marlon Brando, was rumored to show up occasionally, although neither of them had ever seen him, and don't think they didn't look.

Of course, there were the occasional flirtations they dabbled in to satisfy their egos, but it was always agreed they would meet at a certain hour and go home together. There were times when an overzealous he-man with a hyper active ego would give them a hard time, but they made sure to know the bouncer, who would intervene on their behalf, sometimes tossing out the lout with a warning. Other times he would accompany the ladies outside and stuff them into a taxicab if there was a possibility that the would-be suitor might not be able to take *no* for an answer.

The move to Yonkers, and life itself, took its normal turn. It was not long after Carlotta had uttered the words, "I will never set foot in this house again," to Antonia that she and Gloria, soon to be nicknamed the Bobbsey Twins, showed up uninvited to Sunday dinner. Both of them now sporting eggplant-colored hair.

# ∼Thirteen ∼

Joaquín, known as El Bobo, sat watching cartoons in the living room, unfazed by the sea of strangers who came and went from his apartment. Each one of them readily unloaded their problems, hoping Doña Esperanza would have a magic cure. Scores of them paraded into the apartment believing they had been cursed or their children had been cursed by a jealous rival, a distant relative or the devil himself. They desperately sought special prayers, amulets, potions, *anything* that would relieve them of their burdens. There were some who were so frightened of Esperanza's powers and the stories they had heard about her use of them that they came accompanied by reassuring friends and family once their own desperate attempts at ridding themselves of supernatural evils had failed. As Esperanza's powers grew, so did the exaggerations of those same powers.

Doña Esperanza could cure epilepsy, she had made children fly. A wart had grown on a lying woman's tongue, a cripple was made to walk again. She could make you fertile; she could make you sterile. She had found a missing runaway-child, she could speak to the dead. She had even caused an earthquake in Chile. Everyone had a story to tell, and tell them they did.

There was the tale of the married woman who, upon hearing from Doña Esperanza that her husband was having an affair with her own sister, spat at Esperanza, calling her a lying witch, only to find her hair falling out in clumps that very same evening. And there was the man who threatened Esperanza with a kitchen knife after one of her spirits commanded him to stop molesting his nephew, an act he denied vehemently before he lapsed into a coma a few days later, never to regain consciousness again. The latter two happenings did in fact occur, but they were not the work of Esperanza. Regardless of the positive or negative outcomes of Esperanza's treatments and incantations, she had sworn to obey only God from the moment he touched her with his awesome power. In no way did she see her powers as her own; she was only a vehicle or channel for God's actions.

One by one the desperate marched through her tiny railroad apartment, seeking cures and better outcomes, and one by one Doña Esperanza obliged them all. She never asked for remuneration, for that would surely dissipate her powers. Any exchange of money was forbidden, except for the purchase of specific items, some from as far away as Haiti that were needed to effect a given cure.

The door was open to everyone, with the exception of those disgraceful people who wanted to put spells on prospective lovers or on the wives of prospective lovers. These "*idiotas*," as Esperanza referred to them, were quickly shown the other side of the door and told they should be ashamed of themselves. There were plenty of charlatans who were willing to work these despicable curses, but Esperanza was not one of them. She knew that this particular type of black magic inevitably ended in disaster once the truth surfaced, which it always did.

Having cleansed herself at the end of her sessions, Doña Esperanza and El Bobo would clean the apartment with ammonia and holy water, making sure to oust any spirits that may have chosen to linger where they didn't belong. Esperanza had her own evil spirits to battle, one dark one in particular whom she had seen hovering over her daughter Amada ever since the young couple had gone to Puerto Rico for their honeymoon.

# ~ FOURTEEN ~

BACK IN THE CASTLE HILL section of the Bronx, Antonia and Pepitón were engaged in solving their own problem: they had to get the upstairs apartment ready for Amada and Alberto before they returned from the Isle of Enchantment. They had finally gotten Che and Carlotta settled in Yonkers. Now, a new phase in their lives would begin, and it was important to start off on the right foot.

There were many arrangements to be made, but Pepitón put his foot down when Antonia mandated that everything in the upstairs apartment should look identical to the downstairs apartment.

"Ay, Antonia, don't suffocate them! They have their own taste," he said in exasperation, and repeated it every time she chose to do something that was obviously more to *her* liking than that of their son or their new daughter-in-law.

Even so, Pepitón bit his tongue before telling her that her taste had become old-fashioned. "Maybe we should wait and let them pick out their own furniture?"

"And where are they going to sleep when they get back?" she argued. "On the floor?"

"Uh, no . . . " he tried to reason with her, "but they can use the folding bed until they pick out a bedroom set themselves."

"And what are they going to eat, Cheerios every day?" she went on. "Because that seems to be all that your brother and Carlotta left them. They took everything—even the Band-Aids! What if one of them cuts themself. What will they do? Can you tell me *that*?"

It was all he could do not to tell her, *They could always come downstairs for a Band-Aid, if and whenever they find themselves wounded or in need of an ambulance.* He had told himself over and over that silence was the best policy when it came to dealing with Antonia, and for the most part he took his own advice.

What they did do was stock the kitchen with a ton of food, because Alberto would no doubt be starving by the time they arrived. Antonia decided that they needed lots of *plátanos*, as if they wouldn't have had their fill of *tostones* and *mofongo* in Puerto Rico.

"Pepitón, don't forget to bring a bunch of *plátanos* and lots of rice from the *bodega* before they get here."

By the time the newlyweds returned, the upstairs apartment showed no trace of anyone having lived there before, save for the folding bed in the middle of the living room, a new broom behind the kitchen door and a mop and bucket in the corner of the kitchen, in case Antonia had missed a spot. There was also a picture of Doña Antonia's namesake, St. Anthony, hanging in the hallway.

Doña Antonia and Pepitón had so many questions to ask, but there was one immediate question they needed to address: "What happened to your eyes?"

Amada's eyes had turned violet from their previous hazel. She had no idea what had happened to them and assumed she had taken too much sun or something of that nature. Antonia thought she should see a doctor right away, but Amada insisted it wasn't anything serious. Besides, Alberto thought his wife was even more beautiful now that she had violet eyes.

With that said, Pepitón insisted they let the newlyweds rest, and he and Antonia decided to turn in for the evening themselves.

# ~Fifteen~

"No man wants to sleep in a pink bedroom!" was the bell that sounded, when Amada decided to change the color of the bedroom to rose. The first round in what was to become the mother—or to put it into greater perspective—the mother-*in-law* of all battles. Antonia had fired the first shot and followed it up with volley after volley, giving Amada very little time to take cover.

It was not that Amada was a pushover. She had a strong will of her own, which could be attested to by her mother—Doña Esperanza had warned her over and over again not to move into that house. Amada rarely listened to the woman who raised her with all of her silly superstitions, and she was glad to be on her own with a new husband and a new life. It had not been easy being the daughter of a witch, but she was in no way prepared for the problems she would face now that she had become the daughter-in-law of a bitch.

Antonia's disapproval began with the color of the bedroom walls and never stopped. It quickly spread to every stick of furniture Amada chose. For Doña Antonia, the living room furniture was too light. The bedroom furniture was too dark. The dresser was much too big, the night tables too square and the bed, was much too small to allow for two grown people to get a decent night's sleep. The sofa, with its flowery print, too gaudy. The dinnerware, too delicate to be useful. The antiques looked *too* old and shabby. Other new items, too modern. The wallpaper in the bathroom with the naked cherubs was disgraceful, and "Where did they hang the picture of St. Anthony that used to grace the hallway?"

"Why on earth do they need a piano? Neither of them play the piano. It's just a waste of Alberto's hard-earned money," Antonia complained to Pepitón.

She left no doubt that her son worked harder than any man on this earth, present company included. The fact that the piano was an old upright that had belonged to Amada all of her life made no difference to Antonia. It did come as a shock to Antonia, however, and on the very evening that she had uttered those words, to hear a lovely tune played on that very same piano.

"Well," as Pepitón put it, "You really know very little about our son's wife."

"Oh shut up, old man."

When Amada prepared her first meal for Alberto, which consisted of veal cutlets and spaghetti, she was quickly told by her mother-in-law that Alberto hated Italian food and would only eat it to spare her feelings. No matter that Alberto complimented the dinner, like any person who was brought up with good manners by his mother would do. Never to be contradicted Antonia had cooked for him all of his life and she knew for a fact that he did not now and would not ever like anything but Spanish food. What he did love was *arroz con pollo* and *ropa vieja*, which of course should always be accompanied by the ubiquitous black beans, which no meal would be complete without. The fact that Amada did not spoon a little sugar and vinegar into the beans for one of the all-too-frequent family dinners nearly drove Antonia into hysterics.

Amada's clothing was much too suggestive. Now that she was a married woman, Antonia lectured, she should learn to dress down, for it wasn't proper to look desirable in the eyes of other men. There was no need for a decent young woman to show off her figure, and a nice housedress would be much more becoming.

Her make-up? Well, perhaps a little bit of rouge to give her sickly, pale cheeks a touch of color, but lipstick and eye shadow were for floozies. Why anyone would want to paint a line which gave the eyes an "Asian" look was totally unfathomable to Antonia. Of course, other decent enough women painted themselves up in this ridiculous fashion, but *they* were not married to *her* son.

The criticism went on and on until the metamorphosis of Amada was complete. In a very short time she became a smaller, thinner clone of Antonia, leaving Alberto to mourn the disappearance of the beautiful young woman he had married. It did not take long for him to regain his roving eye and begin to look elsewhere for a night of pleasure.

He had what could be called the Peter Pan syndrome: he had not matured and, despite that manly appearance, was still a child inside. And he remained that way, like so many men do when they are forced into marriage too quickly, which was what his mother thought all along. Doña Antonia was of the school that a girlfriend should wait as long as she can, no matter how long that might be, for the male to finally insist on marriage rather than ever thinking he was pushed into it. Had Antonia not waited for Pepitón to come around on his own? Had she pushed, he would have wiggled his way out of the marriage immediately.

"I never heard such a thing," he protested as Antonia expressed her belief that men had to be coaxed into marriage until they thought it was their idea, not the woman's, even though it was. Then he thought to himself, *If I had only known, I might have escaped my current lot in life.* But then again, he really did love her, in spite of her ways. Deep down, he knew he had chosen the right woman.

Pepitón was brought up being lazy, and he would have been lazy to this day had Antonia not pushed him to go farther with his life. He never would have bought the *bodega* if she didn't insist he could do it. He had no idea the hard work that went with that purchase, but she was there every step of the way, cheering him on. He would never have finished high school, if she didn't insist that no one of her stature would marry someone without that diploma. He would never have purchased a house, which he was now *so* proud of, had she not pushed him into it.

As far as Alberto was concerned, Pepitón knew she would do the same for their *hijo adorado*. Pepitón just hoped Amada would not get in the way and let Antonia complete the task of being an excellent mother, even if she was overbearing at times. Pepitón's theory was: *Let Antonia do all the work; my son's wife can do the tweaking afterwards.* Never did it dawn on him that different women have different ideas about these things and he should mind his own business.

# ～Sixteen ～

As Amada tossed her breakfast into the white enamel toilet bowl, her first thought was of Dr. Montalvo, the butcher of a doctor who performed cheap abortions for the neighborhood. This was not the first time she had suffered morning sickness. All the prayers she had uttered in hopes of regaining her period seemed to dissipate in the ether.

She should not have let Alberto and his mother talk her out of going back to school. She should not have let Alberto and his mother talk her out of getting a job. She should not have let Alberto and his mother talk her out of taking birth control pills and she definitely should not have let herself become pregnant.

Staring at the stranger she saw reflected in the mirror, she wondered who had possessed her and why were they using her body to achieve their wicked ends. There were millions of women on this earth who wanted children, and yet *she* was the one chosen to bear a child. It was not that she did not want children, it was that she did not want children at this particular time in her life.

Perhaps she would have felt differently if Alberto had not decided to become a "son of a bitch" so soon into their marriage. He had taken to coming home late every night, claiming to be extremely tired from the hard work he did all day, and only desiring her when his breath reeked of too many beers. It was bad enough that he had trouble avoiding the furniture as he stumbled over his own feet, but what made it worse was that he was a mean drunk who used alcohol as an excuse for his cowardly acts. His drunken antics brought on loud arguments, which were inevitably followed by a grilling session from Antonia the next morning. And in those sessions, Amada always came out the villain, for Antonia's son had never taken to drinking before their marriage. This unusual behavior of his was most likely due to the fact that he was terribly unhappy with something that Amada must have done.

"Besides, a man has to have some time of his own. He works all day and needs to relax once in a while," Antonia would repeat over and over to Amada and to herself, but never out loud where Pepitón might hear.

Amada had not seen her own mother in quite a while and decided it was as good a time as any to visit her. Doña Esperanza had said she would never set foot in that "Godforsaken" house, and to date she had kept her word, despite numerous protests from her only daughter. She was a stubborn old woman who seemed to have a knack for being right. "Thanks to God and the good spirits that surround me," she would repeat many times in her life.

Amada had avoided her mother since returning from the honeymoon because she did not want to explain the changed color of her eyes to Esperanza, but she couldn't keep putting it off. Amada expected Joaquín to come knocking on the door any day now to tell her how wrong it was not to let Esperanza know she was all right. But how could she explain that her eyes had changed color to this woman? It was easy to blame it on the sun to Antonia, but her mother was another story. She believed everything came from the evil thoughts of others. If she *sneezed* it was someone wishing her harm. If her stomach hurt, where did she eat and why? Why couldn't she be just like other girls and get sick once in a while, without someone having wished it on her? Esperanza always thought the worst and, for the most part, she was right.

Amada did not want to face the multitude of questions she would be asked by Antonia upon leaving, so she left by the back entrance—only to find the woman throwing out her garbage as usual. It seemed that whenever Amada decided to go shopping or just take a walk, she was inevitably confronted by Antonia throwing out some sort of rubbish. How two people could accumulate such an abundance of trash astonished Amada, who had no idea that Antonia listened for every move and, when she heard Amada's door close, would grab anything in sight, pretending it needed discarding. It was customary to see a broken lamp or toaster neatly placed into one of the tin cans behind the house, only for that same lamp or toaster to magically return to life and regain its place in the house.

Amada answered all of her questions with falsehoods, not because she had anything to hide, but because she felt that what she did was no one's business but her own. Of course she would never say that out loud, but it was abundantly clear to Antonia, who gritted her teeth and told her not to be late, because her son was used to having dinner at a decent hour. As she walked away, Amada caught, through the corner of her eye, the sight of Antonia retrieving the "broken" radio she had just deposited into the garbage can.

# ⌒ SEVENTEEN ⌒

CLIMBING THE STAIRS to her mother's apartment, Amada could smell the stench of the dirty mop that had been used to clean the hall floors mingling with the aromas of roast pork and gefilte fish. It was a familiar smell that wafted through the tenement building, where a clean bucket of water never seemed to be found by the janitor. She could feel the nausea rising in her throat. She held her breath while the yellow-toothed man grumbled at her for making him pass the dirty mop back over her wet footprints.

Being met at the door by El Bobo, who was on his way to do an errand for Esperanza, Amada was glad to find the parlor free of the countless faces she had grown accustomed to seeing there at all hours. There was no one asking for a special salve for their baby's blisters or an ointment for their arthritis or a lucky prayer to help them hit a number. The only person in that usually crowded apartment was Esperanza, who waved her into the kitchen as she finished mumbling an almost silent prayer and closed her Evangelio. She had asked everyone to leave because she was told by her spirits that Amada would be on her way to see her, and she wanted to be alone with her daughter and the evil spirit who would be accompanying her.

Esperanza began to tremble at first and then broke into what could have been misinterpreted as an epileptic seizure. The dark spirit that attached itself to her daughter seemed to envelop the room, causing Esperanza to lose her ability to breathe. Her guide quickly overtook her tongue, questioning the ominous figure who refused to tell her who he was. It was clear he was a man, but why he followed Amada was not to be discovered on that day or for years to come.

After the prayers and the *pasos* with water and Amada's promise to wear the little medal of St. Michael around her neck—a promise which both women knew would not be kept—mother and daughter visited with each other over coffee as the apartment lightened up for a moment and they were able to bring each other up to date on their lives.

Esperanza knew that Amada was pregnant but feigned ignorance of the little girl that was to be her granddaughter. Instead, she allowed Amada to give her the news and acted convincingly surprised, or so she thought (as if her daughter didn't know her by now). Amada, who was usually closed-mouthed about her private life, seemed to come alive for the moment while telling her mother the reasons for not wanting a child. Esperanza rebuked her, stating, "This too shall pass," and recounted the familiar saga of the many hours of labor she had endured and the sacrifices she had made in order to assure her daughter a healthy, wonderful life.

It had not been easy for Esperanza, especially having been a widow who had not yet found El Bobo to assist her. She stitched hems and altered clothing for people of fluctuating sizes, all the while inhaling the terrible fumes of the dry cleaning establishment where she worked. This did not include the little party dresses that she worked on into the wee hours in order to purchase material for her own daughter's little dresses, which were originals and not purchased in department stores like those worn by "less fortunate little girls." And what about her crooked fingers caused by sewing tiny little sequins, one at a time, onto the communion veil that Sister Teresa removed from Amada's head, replacing it with something less ostentatious?

"Didn't all of this sacrificing account for anything? And Joaquín? Didn't he count for anything either?"

What other man did Amada know who would sacrifice everything for them? It wasn't an accident that brought him to their home so many years ago. He loved them both as he had never loved anyone and he made it his life's work to make them happy, no matter what it took. It was a fact that the only time he argued with Esperanza was when he had wanted to adopt Amada. Esperanza put her foot down; Amada would keep her father's name, no matter the cost, because Esperanza would not be like other women who named their children after different father after different father, never thinking about how that affected the children themselves. Joaquín understood, having three brothers with different last names. He had worked hard all of his life, and the fact that he was a little slower than most men did not stop his goodness from shining through. He sacrificed for them and asked nothing in return.

"You name me one other man who would do that," Esperanza asked, almost daring her to answer.

Amada knew that she couldn't answer honestly without telling her mother what a creep Alberto had become, so she kept silent. The last thing she wanted to hear was, "I told you so." Rather than risk an argument, neither of them said anything about Alberto, nor was the color of Amada's eyes mentioned.

Having run out of conversation, Esperanza brought out an album of old pictures. They both laughed at hairstyles and clothing that had become old-fashioned very quickly.

"Did I really wear my hair up like that?" Amada gasped at one of the photos.

"Yes, you did. You said it was the style, but I never liked it."

"How could you let me go out looking like that?"

"I had to let you grow up, like it or not." Esperanza closed the book and said, "You can't blame me for allowing you to do what you wanted."

Joaquín entered at the designated hour he was to return, coughing loud so he could be heard, not wanting to scare them. They continued to talk for an hour or so, and then Amada, seeing it had become late, said her goodbyes and found herself leaving the apartment in a much better mood than when she had entered.

By the time Amada returned home, with Antonia peeking through the blinds, she had swallowed the sufficient amount of guilt necessary to understand that there would be no visit to Dr. Montalvo, now or ever.

## ～ Eighteen ～

"*Surprise! Surprise!*" Gloria and Carlotta had come to pay Amada a visit and, more importantly, to check out the rumor that she might be pregnant.

The boys, Pedro and Che, were downstairs playing poker with Pepitón and Alberto while Antonia was busy cleaning up after Sunday dinner. The girls had offered to help but had been whisked out of Antonia's kitchen and told to watch television instead. Both women decided this was as good a time as any to keep Amada company, since she didn't feel well and had declined the usual dinner invitation. They thought this was very brave of her, considering the fact that she was not deathly ill or quarantined at home by the New York City Board of Health.

They found Amada looking very healthy indeed, and, if they were not mistaken, she had gained a few pounds since they last saw her. After a million questions, followed by unsatisfactory answers, they begged Amada to tell them the truth. They both knew what pregnant women looked like, the round face Amada had acquired was a dead giveaway, not to mention the fact that she could no longer button her skirt.

Once sworn to secrecy, on the bodies of their mothers and their mother's mother, Amada finally gave in and told them what they had known all along. It was made evident that their screeches of joy were not welcome in the kitchen downstairs when Antonia began banging pots and pans in disapproval. It was not so much the noise that bothered Antonia as the fact that someone else might be having a good time without her. The thought that the hyenas upstairs could be talking about her also crossed her mind, which didn't help the silverware much either.

When Gloria and Carlotta finally rejoined their husbands, it was obvious that each one of them had swallowed a canary and were not about to spill the beans to Antonia. She, in turn, immediately developed a headache and ended the boys' card game, sending everyone home with Che ahead by three dollars. After saying goodbye, Pepitón went into the bathroom and took two aspirins to prepare himself for what was in store: Antonia's headache soon would be his.

The short drive up the Bronx River Parkway in Pedro's new Ford lasted an interminably long time because of traffic. The two women kept rolling their eyes and smiling their secret at each other through the mirror on the visor. When the trio on the radio sang the words *"Yo tengo un secreto,"* Gloria demanded Pedro pull the car over because she was about to wet her pants, which of course he didn't and which of course she did. After a short exchange of a few *carambas* and *idiotas,* Pedro was able to exit the parkway and search for the nearest gas station. While the girls accompanied each other to the ladies' room, which doubled as the men's room, Pedro muttered a few curse words while rubbing a wet paper towel on the car seat in an effort to salvage his stained upholstery.

Once in the ladies room, the women carped about the way men always missed their mark when urinating. What was so hard about pointing and shooting? They *had* to miss just so women using the bathroom would have to straddle the bowl, missing it themselves half the time. "It's not like we have something to point at the bowl with. We end up peeing all over ourselves. Disgusting."

It was not long after the couples had said their goodbyes in the elevator and entered their respective apartments that Pepitón was answering phone calls from his two brothers, whose wives had told them the good news, as soon as each was out of earshot of the other of course. Even Che, deaf as he was, managed to hear the word "pregnant" and convey the message in what sounded like a child's game of Telephone.

Antonia was furious at the fact that she wasn't the first to know. She made no attempt to hide the news from Alberto, who was both stunned and annoyed that *he* wasn't the first to know. It was only Pepitón who broke open the special bottle of Barrilito rum he had been saving since their last trip to the island and toasted the fact that he was about to become a grandfather. He had dreamed of having another child, one that he would take much more responsibility in raising. Although he loved Alberto, he disapproved of his upbringing at Antonia's hands. She simply doted on Alberto too much, and there had been nothing Pepitón could have done to change that. Antonia gave Alberto everything he wanted.

"That is not good for anyone," he often said. "He has got to earn what he gets, or he'll grow up lazy, like I did."

Antonia would have no part of this conversation. In her mind, Alberto was perfect, and that was the end of it.

Pepitón knew that if his son ever got into a fight, he would never have a chance. A boy has to learn how to protect himself. What was Antonia going to do, fight all of his battles for him? His grandson would be different. There would be no coddling where he was concerned. This time, Pepitón would show him the ropes.

It was great to dream. No one could take his dreams from him, not even Antonia.

## ~ Nineteen ~

THE LARGE, EMERALD-GREEN SHAMROCK painted on the window of Clark's Bar belied the fact that most of the patrons of the establishment were of Hispanic origin. It was only on rare occasions that an Irishman entered the premises, usually to ask for directions or to use the men's room. One exception was Officer Houlihan, who made his presence known once a week when he came to collect the envelope that was placed under his shot glass instead of a napkin. Every Thursday at six o'clock, he would repeat the ritual of removing his cap, pretending to wipe his brow, slipping the envelope into his cap and retuning it to cover his neatly cut, bright red hair.

Although Domínguez, the current owner of the bar, resented participating in this illicit transaction, he knew that it was better than having to put up with irate customers confronting tow truck operators who magically appeared to hook up their cars for non-existent parking violations. And every Thursday at six o' five, the men in the bar went through their usual criticism of the entire police force and of Domínguez for being a coward, knowing that each of them would do the same, in similar circumstances. More than one of them had been guilty of slipping an envelope here and there when they wished to work on Sundays, knowing it was against the law to do so.

Since Domínguez had purchased his "American Dream", he had made no changes to the bar, except for the Latin music in the jukebox, most of it performed by one trio or another that, with the exception of Los Panchos, pretty much all sounded the same. There were a couple of *boleros*, one by Tito Rodríguez and the other by Lucho Gatica, but these were usually selected by an occasional female patron accompanying her husband after a movie. The other patrons would be very respectful but were glad when the couple would leave and they could be themselves again with their favorite background music.

This was a man's bar with no frills. There was no pool table and no pinball machine, which would only have served as an invitation to punks and troublemakers. There were no ferns or "No Smoking" signs, which would have been ignored anyway. Neither were there signs stating that shoes must be worn, for what man in his right mind would walk around the city streets that were covered with spit and dogshit in his bare feet? But most importantly, there was no one there to snitch to their wives that they had taken a detour on the way home, which they would drunkenly deny on their mother's honor once they finally did arrive home. The men were there to drink and unwind after a day's work, and it was clear that women were not welcome.

No one considered Mary, the grey-haired lady who came in nightly for her three Bloody Marys, a woman. She didn't flirt with anyone or start fights among them and, more importantly, she was not acquainted with any of their wives. She had patronized the bar with her husband before he died, "God bless his soul," and she would continue to patronize it until their reunion someday in heaven.

The men were there to play cards and dominoes and an occasional number with the runner who dropped in not so casually each evening. Every now and then, the numbers man would pay off on a dream, a license plate number or a child's birthday. Only once had one of the more brilliant *compañeros* come up with the idea of putting money on Houlihan's badge number, an idea that mushroomed into a wonderful omen—only to cost them all a great deal of money. After losing their shirts, the brilliant one was never allowed to forget it, and was hence known as *el gran pendejo.*

Occasionally, one of their wives would show up, and the men would turn into the three monkeys of hear, speak and see no evil, which would infuriate the wife as she headed toward the bathroom (the place where they all went to hide from their wives) to retrieve her husband by the ear and drag him home. "You should be spending your money on your children instead of throwing it away in a bar," she would yell, as everyone agreed with her while hiding their faces in their jackets or behind one another to avoid recognition. When she was gone, they would tell each other how glad they were she wasn't *their* wife. The really tough ones would say, "If that was my wife, she'd know better. She'd never get away with that and still have teeth." Something they all knew was not true.

It was only when Sarah came up on the scene that the atmosphere seemed to change and a sense of discomfort overcame them. The jokes they told were not as loud or raunchy. They each resented having to shake their heads furiously to Domínguez as he held up the phone, asking whether they were there or not, instead of yelling to him, to the delight of their buddies, to tell "the *vieja*" they hadn't been there all day. It also put them at a disadvantage when one of "the *viejas*" did show up to escort them home. It was just too difficult to explain that they had no interest in Sarah, the out-of-place young woman, who *of course* they didn't find attractive.

It didn't take the collective mind of these geniuses to realize the reason for her nightly visits. She had zeroed in on Alberto, who had become a semi-regular and who pretended to be surprised to see her as he bought her a drink and joined her at one of the tables. After witnessing this scene a few times the men shrugged their shoulders in a live-and-let-live attitude and the chance meetings soon became as routine as the usual drinks they ordered. This little song and dance was never performed when Pedro accompanied his nephew to Clark's Bar. That was when Sarah would find herself sitting alone, only once in a while fending off an attempt to hit on her by someone who had had enough to drink and hadn't heeded the warnings of his *compadres*. Alberto would fidget in Uncle Pedro's presence and pretend not to know her while mouthing "I'm sorry" to her when he had the chance.

It was only when Pedro would show up unexpectedly that Alberto would jump up from the table with some meager excuse, only to be reminded by Pedro that he was the husband of a pregnant wife who loved him very much and who was a very good woman, unlike a lot of other women he could name. This was stated loud enough for the entire bar to hear, but it seemed to make no difference to Sarah, the intended target of his words. She would just smile, infuriating him even further. Pedro believed in the sanctity of marriage and was determined to see that his nephew followed his good teachings.

Perhaps if the woman weren't so brazen and didn't act so whorish, perhaps then he would have understood the attraction she held for Alberto. Never did it occur to him that witchcraft was involved. To Pedro, there was no reason on earth for Alberto to go sneaking around with someone who had obviously been around the block a few times. Pedro took to watching his nephew like a hawk, rarely letting him out of his sight. When he sent Alberto on an errand for the gas station, he would check his watch, making certain that his nephew understood he was being timed. He was angry at the role he was given to play, and more than once he thought of telling his brother about his suspicions, but he too belonged to the good old boys club that took a silent vow at birth never to tell on one of their own. He could not even speak to his wife Gloria about it, because he knew his suspicions would be broadcast to the world within minutes. He toyed with the idea of giving his nephew a swift kick in the pants. However, then he would have to contend with Antonia, who would no doubt make him miserable for the rest of his life for even thinking her son could do wrong. Instead, he opted for silence, hoping this unsavory affair would soon pass.

# ⁓ TWENTY ⁓

THE METAMORPHOSIS that overtook Antonia was remarkable. After the initial shock and anger she had experienced at not being the first to learn the news of the impending birth of her first grand-child, she became the doting mother-in-law, playing the part to the hilt. Amada, the dear, young mother-to-be, could do no wrong. She became the daughter Antonia never had. The urge to grab a broom and bang on the ceiling had dissipated. It no longer irritated Antonia when she heard the piano tinkling from the upstairs apartment. In fact, she encouraged Amada to play, for it was good for the baby, who no doubt would have musical incli-nations himself someday. There was no doubt in her mind that the child would be a boy, because she knew her son came from a fam-ily with strong genes.

When Amada stated that she really didn't mind being alone, Antonia wouldn't hear of it and insisted that she accompany her and Pepitón to the *bodega* each day, "not to work, mind you," but to rest. It was not good for a woman in Amada's condition to not be around people, just in case the baby had a mind of its own. No grandchild of *hers* would be born in the back of a taxi or a police car.

Pepitón enjoyed his new wife, whose familiar frown had been replaced with a smile, something that seemed foreign on her face and took some effort on his part not to laugh at.

Even with this change in personality, she was not immune to mockery; it was her singing that he and his customers could have done without. Although her voice was naturally deep, she insisted on singing two octaves higher than what anyone considered to be normal. The domino players re-stationed themselves in front of Kay's knitting store rather than anyone have their portable radio compete with the shrill tones emanating from the *bodega*.

Pepitón shook his head in wonderment as he noticed his wife wore a bit more make-up than usual, and her clothes too were a little more colorful and less baggy. But his greatest shock came one quiet Sunday evening at home after the dinner guests had left, when she reintroduced him to her dance of seduction. He had long forgotten that look in his wife's eyes, and initially it frightened him, but after a quick drink and a slow *bolero*, he saw the woman who had aroused his passions so many years earlier, and he felt himself seduced by her charms.

It had been ages since they had been intimate with each other. Although there was awkwardness to their passion, they both felt fulfillment and vowed the next time would be better. As Pepitón lay awake that night, he could not help but feel he had taken advantage of someone who had obviously lost her mind.

There was a new life beginning for the entire family, and Antonia seemed to enjoy that fact most of all. Each evening she would sift through the newspapers for sales, and the next morning after restocking the store shelves, replacing the old loaves with new bread and making sandwiches for the teenagers on their way to school and their parents on their way to work, she would force a not-too-reluctant Amada to accompany her to Alexander's to buy a new maternity frock or some other gift for the baby. It was never too early to purchase booties or diapers or a crib or a layette. It was better to be prepared and not have to rush everything at the last minute.

When Amada balked at listening to the spiel of an encyclopedia salesman, she was reminded that all children should have the benefit of the best education, especially Antonia's grandson, who would no doubt be reading before he learned to walk. After all, her son Alberto had recited his ABCs while he was still in the cradle. When Pepitón decided to take his life into his own hands by reminding his wife that their son was not even potty-trained until he was old enough to wear long pants, he was glad that she had discarded her old habit of throwing the nearest object she could find at him, especially since she was dangerously close to a marble ashtray that could cause great damage to a human body. He was pilloried with, "You buffoon, you would know I'm telling the truth if you had paid more attention to your son than you did to a racing form." Having been reminded of a time, long since forgotten, when he had almost lost his home and his marriage, he quickly recognized that Antonia's idea of purchasing the encyclopedia was nothing short of inspired.

The next item on Antonia's agenda was an absolute surprise to Amada. Anything modern had always been out of the question, but now she insisted that Amada dress especially nice for Alberto. It was time she "dressed like the other young women around the block." What she had thought of as a little too whorish for her daughter-in-law she now found just right for the mother-to-be. No more silly housedresses for Amada, she was much too young for that nonsense. So it was off to Alexander's again.

"Try this one on," she said as Amada tried on dress after dress, until she was worn out from the ordeal. "Buy one for before and one for after," she urged until Amada gave up and couldn't try on another thing. After all, no woman was ready to try on a whole new wardrobe in one day. "Buy, buy, buy," had become Antonia's motto, and she was enjoying it to the fullest. She had never spent money on herself, and now she was charging like a lunatic. Pepitón could afford it. "What was he going to do?

Take all his money to the grave?" The shopping spree ended only when Amada promised she would return the following day. And return they did until Amada's wardrobe was complete, including a pair of stylish pumps she found a bit daring, but Antonia convinced her that she wore the very same style pump when she was younger.

Now that Antonia had finished with one problem, it was time to face the other, even if it meant breaking her heart.

~ ~ ~

"*M'ija*, it's getting late," Pepitón said to Antonia as he handed her a cup of coffee. "Don't you think you should come inside?"

"I'll be in in a little while. You go finish watching your cowboys."

"Okay," he said, shrugging his shoulders as he headed inside. "Just don't stay out here too late."

Antonia paced in and out of the house, waiting to see Alberto's car pull into the driveway. Although she never allowed a hint of criticism where her son was concerned, she was angered by the fact that he was taking too long to come home. She had formed the questions she would ask him in her mind a hundred times. When Alberto did arrive, and she saw her prince stumble toward her, she felt sick to her stomach. Antonia said nothing as she raised her hand, as she had never done before, and slapped him hard across the face, making it clear that it was time for him to grow up and become a man.

# ～ TWENTY-ONE ～

IT WAS NOT OFTEN that the family all ventured to Glen Island for a picnic, but now that Che and Carlotta had moved to Yonkers and purchased park passes on the advice of Pedro and Gloria, it was only fair for the people from the Bronx to travel into their territory once in a while.

Antonia sat in the backseat of Che's Ford SUV, waiting for Gloria to finally get her lazy butt downstairs. Pedro had already showed up with a giant bag that he and Che were attempting to fit in the car along with everyone else's belongings. *You would swear we were going for a week instead of a day*, she thought, wondering how they were all going to fit in the one car.

Gloria finally showed her face, but before anyone could issue a complaint, she herself blurted out the reason for her tardiness. "I got cotton in my ears, Monistat in my vagina and a suppository up my ass. I'm good to go."

She shoved herself into the SUV, making sure to sit next to Antonia leaving just enough room for Pedro to get in.

He just smiled at her and said, "Maybe you better go alone. We don't want to spoil the party."

"*No seas tonto, Pedro,*" she replied as she gave him enough room for a linebacker.

As they inched their way through the city streets, Pepitón shook his head, knowing if they took the Hutchinson River Parkway, they would get there in ten minutes instead of the hour drive that was ahead of them. It did him no good to tell Che to take the Parkway. He'd never hear him anyway. He stared at Antonia, who pretended to be interested in Yonkers rather than glare back at him, her indifference meaning "I told you so."

To top it off, when they reached Glen Island, the drawbridge was open and they had to wait until a ship passed. All of this was too much for Antonia, who was ready to go home before the picnic even started.

After finally arriving and staking their claim to a couple of picnic tables and a barbecue pit, the "boys" went fishing with their new poles that never caught anything, while the "girls" lounged around on lawn chairs enjoying a beer or a soda as they watched the sailboats and yachts glide past them on the water. They all agreed it was a beautiful place, although Antonia found nothing wrong with Pelham Bay Park, which was much bigger, a lot more private and only a stone's throw from home.

On this particular day, she balked at the fact that they had chosen tables too near an Italian family, which numbered in the hundreds (twenty-six people, to be exact), who had unloaded more food from their cars than she had in her entire *bodega*. They had partaken of barbecued coffee, bacon, eggs and sausages for breakfast and were now in the process of barbecuing lunch, which included lasagna, chicken, sausage and peppers and pot-loads of various foods she did not even recognize. The women set about preparing the meals while the older husbands took off to play bocce and the younger ones soccer. The smaller children took turns running around a hammock strung between two trees, while their mothers scolded them in "yakkety-yak" Italian for bothering their grandfather, who was fast asleep and oblivious to them all. Antonia could not help but comment derogatorily on how fast they spoke in their foreign language, which was rude of them to begin with, as they in turn found the strains of her "yakkety-yak" Spanish rude also.

The beach at Glen Island, which Antonia let it be known was nothing more than section 14 of Orchard Beach and was apparently fenced off just to keep the Bronxites out, had way too many pebbles in the sand to suit her. It was also much too small and confining, and the well-enforced law that allowed no food on the beach made the people who dug their heads low under blankets for a bite of a peanut butter or cheese sandwich every now and then look like ostriches. Why anyone needed a special pass to a public park and a public beach, especially if they were residents of Westchester County, only to be forced to pay a separate fee for use of the parking lot, was ludicrous to her and surely just another form of snobbery.

It irked Antonia that after paying to use the beach, they could not go into the water because the disgusting horseshoe crabs with their long, pointed tails had decided it was mating season and were all over the water's edge, like giant cockroaches trying to hump each other. The overheated women were forced to sit in the sand like "perspiring beached whales," as Antonia put it. She covered her bulges with a large towel, feeling everyone on the beach was staring at her and thinking, "How can she wear a bathing suit with *that* figure."

Amada, who had rented a collapsible chair which she had to be helped in and out of, had opted for shorts and a maternity blouse because of her distorted figure. Carlotta and Gloria must surely have shopped for their bathing suits in a jungle habitat; they both wore bright colors with what appeared to be peacocks painted on them. Antonia was quick to point out that the bird beaks pointed directly to their vaginal areas, which was not becoming of persons who purported to be ladies.

It was only when a young girl with a pear-shaped figure had the effrontery to sit on a blanket next to theirs, wearing the identical bathing suit Antonia had hidden beneath her towel, that she made a hasty escape back to the picnic area, leaving the others to bask in the sun without the benefit of her unsolicited play-by-play. She did, however, advise Amada to sit beneath a tree for shade in her condition, before making her way back to the dressing area, loudly ouchy-owing at the hot sand under her feet.

It was during this respite that Amada was treated to stereophonic reasons why it was imperative that she choose the peacock on the right or the peacock on the left to be the godmother of the soon-to be-born child, each insisting that they not only had seniority, but they also would take wonderful care of the child in the event of some unforeseen occurrence, which of course would never happen, "but you never know." After a lot of bickering, at which the pear-shaped beauty clicked her teeth and moved conveniently close to a suntanned gigolo with dark glasses, it was decided they would be co-godmothers, thus eliminating any possible hurt feelings.

"If it's a girl, I'll buy the little christening gown she'll wear," Gloria volunteered, quickly taking ownership.

"Who made you the boss?" shot back Carlotta.

"Nobody, but since I have better taste . . . "

"Since when?"

"What if you both pick it out together?" Amada suggested, ending that argument before it started.

Over an hour later, when the women decided they had argued enough and were wrought enough with guilt at having left Antonia, "*la pobrecita*," alone for so long, they finally returned to their barbecue site and were astonished to find Antonia enjoying a glass of vino and a homemade cannoli with the Italian ladies as they respectively yakkety-yakked to each other in their native tongues, exchanging complaints about the weather, cooking and lazy, good-for-nothing husbands who fished or played bocce while they did all the work. These complaints could be understood in any language and could not be misinterpreted as a slight to their husbands, whom they loved very much.

# ～ TWENTY-TWO ～

WHEN DR. MOUND received the call to the maternity ward at Lincoln Hospital he had just listened to the tiny heartbeat which was camouflaged behind the massive belly of Mrs. Pérez, now pregnant with her sixth child. Having ushered her previous five into this world with his gentle hands, he assured her that the new baby would be healthy also and advised her to consider taking a hiatus from the baby-making business for a year or two. After all, everyone needed a vacation once in a while, despite what Mr. Pérez had to say about it.

As he made his apologies to the many pear-shaped women in his waiting room, promising to return as soon as he could, he reminded them that babies did not believe in appointments and arrived whenever they "darn well" pleased.

Dr. Mound had been practicing medicine for over twenty-five years, yet he found himself excited every time a new baby was about to enter the world. He didn't know why he felt this way, he just knew that he was happy about it, and that in turn made his many patients feel the same way. None of his patients ever deserted him for the more upscale doctors, knowing he cared about their babies almost as much as they did.

Earlier that morning on his way to Lincoln Hospital, he looked around and saw how much the neighborhood had changed. What had been Jewish-owned stores with signs saying

"Se Habla Español" now actually did have cashiers that spoke Spanish, and not the broken Spanish that got them through their transactions. Most of his patients were Spanish-speakers of some sort. Some Puerto Rican, some Cuban, some South American, but the one thing they all had in common was when they needed an obstetrician, they all agreed he was the best.

The thought of a *mezuzah* still hanging by the door in many of the apartments that were now inhabited by "Spanish" people made him smile. The new apartment dwellers didn't know what it meant, but they knew it was holy, and that was good enough for them. Jewish or Christian, people with children living in the Bronx knew they needed all of the help they could get.

Passing an ices vendor, Dr. Mound remembered the jelly apples that were hawked in the same stands in his youth. *Nothing changes*, he thought, *just the languages and the foods*.

When he arrived at the hospital he ran smack-dab into a worried Antonia and Pepitón and assured them it would be better for all concerned if they went into the waiting room so he could attend to Amada. They both kept asking him questions, acting like nervous wrecks, until he finally showed them to the waiting room and reminded them what it was there for: "To wait!"

He thought back to this same pair so many years ago, when it was Antonia giving birth and the same Pepitón was nervous as a cat. He had to assure him that mother and son would be fine and in no time he'd have another mouth to feed. Little Alberto was born very quickly, and he knew that these parents were going to spoil him rotten.

What he didn't expect was the look on Amada's face. He was shocked by the brightness of her full set of teeth, which were locked together in an almost frightening grimace. It was an image that would remain with him forever, for never had he seen a mouth that had, what seemed to him, as many teeth as a piano has keys.

Try as he did to relax this mother to be, those teeth remained locked through the breathing, through the screaming, through the grunting, and only relaxed when little Milagros finally popped her head into the world, three hours and twenty-seven minutes later.

After congratulating the mother and both sets of grandparents—for Pepitón had called Esperanza as he had promised Amada he would—Dr. Mound went directly to the bar across the street and ordered himself a double bourbon, something he had never done in his twenty-eight years of practice.

"She's beautiful," they lied to Amada's face.

They all had agreed behind Amada's back that Milagros, the precious angel that slept peacefully in the incubator, was possibly the ugliest child they had ever lain eyes on. Of course all babies were *initially* ugly, considering the ordeal they had to go through, but Milagros was especially odd-looking. She was very long and skinny and had much too much hair enveloping her wrinkled little face.

"She looks like a little baboon," Antonia whispered to Pepitón, who himself wished that God had thought to leave a little more hair on his head and a little less on that of Milagros.

Try as they did, they could find no resemblance in that "little thing" that slept before them to anyone in their family, especially not to Alberto. Antonia and Pepitón immediately agreed that Milagros must have come out looking like someone on her mother's side.

Esperanza's reaction to her granddaughter was also one of disappointment, likening the child to a hairy turnip, as she too, quickly searched her family tree for some small link of recognition, only to come up empty. She did, however, agree with El Bobo when he stated that Milagros looked very much like a miniature, albeit hairy, version of Pepitón. Having absolved themselves of any genetic responsibility for the child's features, they could now go about the business of loving this little angel, who, "thank God," had all ten fingers and ten toes, which both families counted more than once, just to be certain.

When Alberto was finally tracked down by Pedro, he hastened to his wife's side, carrying a large bouquet of gladiolus, Amada's least favorite flower. He also came prepared with a list of excuses for not having been there for the birth of their child. "Yes," he had seen her, and "Yes," she was beautiful and "No," of course he wasn't disappointed that she hadn't given birth to a son, which was a lie easily detected by the immediate clearing of the throat that followed his words.

All of this seemed insignificant to Amada when she took little Milagros in her arms that evening and saw neither baboon nor turnip, but a beautiful daughter who was a true gift from God.

# ⌒ TWENTY-THREE ⌒

PEDRO'S MURDER SHOCKED EVERYONE. He had been busy showing
a young man how simple it was to replace his car filter and did
not see someone slip into the station's office. It was late in the
evening. Alberto had left for the day after a disturbing argument
that Pedro had barely managed to shake from his mind by concen-
trating on his work.

Pedro was also distracted by Sarah, the cause of his argument
with Alberto. His nephew's relationship with that girl bothered
him to no end. Alberto had a beautiful wife and child waiting for
him at home, yet he insisted on having this stupid affair with a tart
of questionable upbringing. Pedro himself had asked her not to
come around and keep Alberto from doing his work, but she paid
no attention to him. She would just snap her gum and say she'd
come around until *Alberto* told her not to come, and that was that,
like it or not. Up to now, there was little Pedro could do to stop
the affair. After all, Alberto was a grown man who knew what he
was doing. He didn't need two fathers to pester him about Sarah.
It had come to the point that Pedro was sorry he had ever agreed
to let Alberto work for him, for no matter what he did or said,
everything turned into an argument.

After waving goodbye to his last customer, Pedro was surprised as he entered the office to find a young man rifling through
the cash register. His immediate reaction was the thought of cuff-

ing the boy on the back of the head as he had done so many times to the kids from the neighborhood who sassed him with their bravado. He was about to accost the intruder until he caught sight of the silver gun in the waistband of the thief's faded khakis.

His intention was to back out unnoticed and let the kid have whatever money there was in the register. Pedro was not a hero and had never thought of becoming one. Besides, *the kid probably needs it more than I do*, he thought, considering the cheap, worn-out sneakers on his feet.

Pedro's footstep on the creaky floorboard brought the gun into the young boy's hand. For the first time in his life, Pedro realized what pure evil looked like as their eyes met. This was no ordinary delinquent, like the *títeres* he had seen hanging around on stoops and street corners, but rather an individual who had long ago made his vow to the devil.

Pedro did as he was told, removing his pants after tossing his keys into the station yard. He was to be humiliated and laughed at for the sake of a few dollars he cared nothing about. He was forced to his knees, kicked like a dog and made to beg for his life by a gold-toothed mouth that kept smiling at him and his pain, occasionally stopping to spit at him.

Perhaps the evening would have ended differently had Pedro not looked up from his knees and seen his beloved Marilyn in her exquisite nakedness witnessing his utter humiliation. It was at that precise moment that Pedro went completely insane. Before the fatal bullet was fired into his heart he sprang forward, grabbed the man's throat and, bit a chunk out of his ear.

Pedro tried to concentrate. He did not understand why he lay there and saw Gloria smile at him. He smiled back. She was dressed in her wedding gown, and he felt proud as a peacock that this beautiful girl had agreed to be his wife. He thought about how lucky he was. He heard Pepitón's words: "Nice going, squirt." And Che playing the trumpet at his wedding. No one could play like his brother. He remembered that he should ask Che to play again, just like old times. He had so much to remember as he smiled and breathed his last breath.

Pedro's murder received no coverage in the English-language newspapers. It was just another insignificant death in the Bronx. The *Diario-La Prensa* sandwiched it between the murders of two other Latinos that had taken place in the city the night before. It was only the funeral cortège, made up of the hundreds of cars Pedro had worked on, that caused traffic to stop as it slowly made its way to Woodlawn Cemetery and made people take notice of the very humble but very important man who had died.

Che and Pepiton could barely stand at the graveside. They were held up by their wives as the priest wafted incense over the casket that would be lowered into the open grave. It was not supposed to be this way. This was their little brother; it was their responsibility that nothing happen to him. Now, they felt useless and ashamed of themselves.

"Why hadn't I done more for him?" Pepitón kept saying. "I should have been there for him. He was my baby brother."

Che said nothing, but the anger on his face was evident. He wanted to fight the world, but he especially wanted to kill the piece of garbage that had killed his brother. The amount of hurt that was present at the funeral would be felt for years to come, but for the brothers, it would last for the rest of their lives.

In another part of the Bronx a woman walked onto the pier, ignoring the two hooky-playing boys who sat fishing as she placed the remains of a black candle shaped like a man into a brown bag containing Pedro's grease-stained handkerchief and tossed it into the East River.

# ∾ TWENTY-FOUR ∾

IT SEEMED THAT GLORIA'S HAIR turned gray overnight. In reality, she had just stopped dyeing it that silly eggplant color and had let it grow out naturally. No one, not even Pedro, knew that she had been prematurely gray from the age of fourteen, after having seen a vision of the Virgin Mary kneeling at the altar next to her in St. Athanasius church. Her mother, who had attributed her vision to the little pamphlets the church gave out in Catechism classes which spoke of the miracles of saints, told her it would be wise never to speak of this hallucination, for she would shame the family and ultimately end up in the loony bin.

Carlotta, who had been turned away from Gloria's door with her offers of chicken soup or *menudo* one time too many, had confided to Che that Gloria's behavior was getting to the point where shock therapy might not be too extreme a measure to take. Carlotta, although sympathetic to Gloria's loss, could not help but feel that she, too, had suffered a loss, the loss of her good friend or as Antonia would say, "her partner in crime." There was no one to shop with or go dancing with or, most importantly, to gossip with. Gloria would not even answer the telephone, even with the secret signal of two rings and a hang up followed by another ring.

What no one realized was that Gloria was feeling the guilt that came from having levied an extraordinary amount of criticism on Pedro when he was alive. She had hated smoking, mostly because the smell of his cigarettes would remain in the curtains and sometimes permeate her clothing. There had been many arguments following her tossing of his cigarette packs into the toilet bowl. She always used the excuse that she worried about his health and that he surely was going to die from the cancer sticks and leave her a grieving widow. His argument that he would be more likely to catch pneumonia from her opening windows in the middle of winter had fallen on deaf ears. In fact, he did develop a terrible cold that had kept him out of work for three days after she had sent him to smoke outdoors on a cold, snowy day. His one feeble attempt at a joke, in which he envisioned her contributing to the death of many fish from flushing nicotine into the ocean, was met with no more than a raised eyebrow and a cluck.

Gloria had criticized the noises he made during lovemaking, which she was sure the neighbors in the upstairs apartment could hear. They always seemed to be dancing a *tarantella* above their heads during their nights of passion. Because Pedro was ever the gentleman, he never let on about the whistling noises *she* made. Instead, lovemaking for Pedro became almost painful. He would hold his breath, trying to be silent, and almost choke to death during climax.

She had criticized his height, his eating habits, his clothing, his dark, grease-stained hands, which were not allowed to touch her until they were scrubbed with cleanser. She hated the way his hand always slipped down to her behind when they danced, and she would always pick it up and put it back on her waist where it belonged. It was definitely his fault that they did not have children; obviously, there was nothing wrong with *her* side of the family, she would repeat more than once. After all, wasn't she the daughter of a woman who bore eleven healthy children?

She was "fed up," as she had put it, with his roving eye. Why else would ladies act so ridiculous when he explained to them the intricacies of a tune-up or an oil change, which was something every woman should know and was not necessary for him to teach, unless he was planning a special kind of tune-up of his own?

It was that same twinkle in his eyes that had made her fall for this "little shrimp" that she loved dearly. She cursed the walls and the ceilings, or wherever he might be, for him having left her alone.

How could she tell Carlotta, her best friend, that she was angry at her husband for dying? That she missed him so much and that there were many times she thought of joining him? Just ending it all. She wouldn't understand. No one would. There was so much pain, and she alone had to deal with it. She had tried to talk to Carlotta, to make her understand what she was going through, but that was something that seemed impossible. She had bitten her tongue more than once rather than say: "How would you feel if Che was to die?" That would be a horrible thing to say, and yet, how else could she make Carlotta understand?

Instead, they talked about silly things. Things she didn't care about at all. Who gave a damn that it might rain or that the sun was shining today? Who cared if there was a good show on television or a good movie that they should go and see? Who cared if there was a good book that she just *had* to read? She wanted to talk about Pedro, and no one wanted to talk about him at all. It was as if he had disappeared and that was that. *Time to live your life and forget he ever existed.*

The knock on the door brought her back to her senses, but she stayed seated and quiet, not wanting to listen to Carlotta ask if she needed anything from the store, something of that nature. Antonia's voice on the other side of that door quickly changed her attitude. She might have been able to ignore Carlotta, but never Antonia. What she didn't understand was that this gruff human being had a side to her she had never seen.

Antonia listened to Gloria as she released all of her rage and misery at having lost Pedro. Gloria spoke of all of the wonderful things he had ever done for her. When she finished, it was Antonia's turn to tell Gloria things she did not know about Pedro, things she had been told by Pepitón about his brother. Foolish things they had done as children, some embarrassing, some silly and some downright ridiculous. They found themselves laughing and crying and wishing they had known the men when they were boys.

Antonia couldn't stop the tears that flowed from her eyes as she recalled the brothers daring Pedro to take a dip in the neighbor's pool. After he removed his clothes the other two ran away with them, leaving Pedro to sneak through the backyards after dark, praying no one would see him.

"*¿Desnudo?*"

"*En pelotas.*"

They laughed so hard that Carlotta, who "just happened to be passing by," thought something was wrong and just *had* to knock on the door to be certain everything was okay. They assured her everything was and invited her in for coffee, which she readily accepted. They then chatted on about everything except Pedro, but Gloria knew she had someone to confide in if things got too rough. By the time Antonia left, it seemed as if the place had gotten brighter, and for some reason Gloria felt she could breathe again.

# ～ TWENTY-FIVE ～

THE TERRIBLE AROMA that emanated from Milagros' carriage brought on the familiar "*¡Fo!*" from Antonia as she changed the child's diaper and decided it was time for Pepitón to take the baby for a walk before they lost any more customers.

Objecting as he was handed his hat and pushed out of the door with the child in the stroller, Pepitón was reminded that he was of no use to them in the *bodega*, since he insisted on insulting every customer who had some complaint. He left Antonia to use what little charms she possessed to keep them from going to the rival *bodega* just down the street by assuring them that "Pepitón was not in his right mind". The baby needed some sun, and she and Amada could handle the store just fine without him.

The domino players had returned to their old set-up in front of the *bodega* after Kay's Knitting Store customers had complained about their inability to knit and purl because of the racket the players' radio made with its odd-sounding music. Pepitón was not happy to receive them and had thrown a pot of cold water on them for cussing and gambling in front of his establishment. This had never bothered him before. He had confiscated a portable radio from a woman with extraordinary-sized breasts when she refused to lower the volume. It was only with the help of Officer Houlihan, who appeared mesmerized by her cleavage, that she was able to retrieve it. Pepitón was surly to the teenagers who came to buy sandwiches, and he reprimanded their parents for being too lazy or too preoccupied with their jobs or their television sets to make the sandwiches themselves.

Antonia realized that her husband was hurting deeply. This man who was once known for his spit and polish would now only shower and shave when he was reminded to do so. On many occasions he showed up at the kitchen table in his underwear, only to be told that he had forgotten to dress. Days would pass when he would not utter a word, leaving Antonia to imagine what frightening images were going through his mind. What worried her most of all, however, was the fact that he was hell-bent on avenging his brother's murder and had secretly purchased a gun illegally. He hid it in a cigar box behind the counter without having first consulted with her.

~ ~ ~

When Pepitón wheeled his granddaughter into St. Mary's Park, he made certain to sit on a bench far away from the babbling mothers who all insisted that their little princesses in pink were the prettiest in the park and their little princes in blue were nothing short of perfection. He was annoyed that no one paid attention to the little boy in the bright red T-shirt, who scampered up and down a large rock on the constant brink of falling and splitting his head. How many times had he warned his little brother Pedro that he could fall from that very same rock before he eventually did, breaking his arm? On that occasion, Pepitón had scooped him up and rushed him to Lincoln Hospital on a breathtaking bicycle ride

"Be careful on that rock. You can hurt yourself," he yelled to the boy.

"Mind your own business."

"Maybe it is my business."

"You're not my father," the boy in the red T-shirt yelled back at him, the same way Pedro had yelled at him a thousand times.

*You're not my father.* The words swirled through his brain as he instinctively grabbed the shins that had been kicked so many times for his interfering in the many fights Pedro had had with the bigger boys who always made fun of his size. He wore his height as a badge of honor, always accepted the challenges of bullies who seemed to think he had been placed on this earth to prove their superiority. And Pedro, more than once, had come out on top. But Pepitón was always there beside him to make sure it was a fair fight.

Pepitón thought back to the day Pedro bought the gas station. How proud he had felt being the owner of something. No one thought it would go anywhere, but he read everything he could about cars. He could tell a customer what was wrong without even looking at the vehicle. Little by little he developed a following of the faithful who would bring their automobiles from as far off as Connecticut or New Jersey to have them checked out or repaired.

As Pepitón shaded little Milagros from the sun he could feel the anger in his chest. Tears streamed down his cheeks at the awareness that he was no longer there to help his brother fight a battle.

It was only when the little boy in the red T-shirt scampered down from the rock and sat down next to him, taking Pepitón's hand to console him, that he realized his brother had forgiven him and would be with him forever.

# ⌒ TWENTY-SIX ⌒

ST. ATHANASIUS CHURCH was filled to capacity when Milagros was christened Milagros María Teresa by Father O'Connor, who had grown red in the face after having to repeat everything over and over again to Che, the godfather who heard nothing, and Carlotta, the godmother who had trouble remembering what she was supposed to say or do. The front pews were occupied by many proud members of the family, all dressed in their Sunday best, while several spectators sat in the back rows, dressed in black as they waited for the service to start for their dearly departed friend or relative, who was forced to remain outside in the hearse until this extended baptismal ritual ended.

Alberto and Amada were very proud of their little girl, who giggled as the holy water was poured over her forehead, rather than cry as most babies did. Her dark hair was tied with a beautiful white-laced satin ribbon, which matched the lovely outfit that Doña Esperanza had sewn for her, in spite of the fact that Doña Antonia thought it would be more appropriate for her to wear the beautiful little outfit she had seen in Lord & Taylor. Milagros, whose face had finally grown into her features, had become a very pretty child, and she continued to giggle as she was carried out of the church past the six very old men who struggled up the stairs with a coffin. The weeping that accompanied the mourners did not faze Milagros one bit. She realized, from all of the attention she was receiving, that she was the star attraction.

Everyone, at least everyone invited, showed up to celebrate at Pepitón and Antonia's house, including El Bobo and Esperanza, who had to be coaxed and cajoled into coming by both Alberto *and* Amada. They had finally threatened to never speak to the two grandparents again if they didn't share in the happiness of this great event. Doña Esperanza, whose excuses ranged from arthritis to not having a thing to wear to bunions finally succumbed to their arguments, but only if she would be permitted to change into slippers once she arrived. She reminded her daughter that she hated dressing up and wearing heels, and this would be a great sacrifice for her.

Many of the guests, who hadn't seen each other since Pedro's funeral, had difficulty finding the house because Antonia had insisted on having it painted a pale yellow in time for the christening. Pepitón, who was dubbed "Jack Benny" by Antonia because of his stinginess, had decided that it would be less expensive if he, Alberto and Che painted the house themselves. This of course turned into a fiasco as the house continued to swallow the gallons of paint they brushed on it. Eventually, after Che fell off of the roof, not heeding the warning from Alberto that he had moved the ladder, the work was left to professionals. It ended up costing, as Pepitón quoted to everyone, "an arm and a leg."

Although invited, Ding Ding, the freeloader, sent his regrets, after hearing from one person too many about the great amount of food and champagne he had consumed at Alberto and Amada's wedding and only placing ten dollars in the envelope. Ding Dong was deemed *persona non grata* after insisting on taking photographs at the wake, which he assured everyone was a proper thing to do as he was being tossed out of the funeral parlor. The same status was given to Chicha, who had made a spectacle of herself at the gravesite by threatening to jump into the grave behind

Pedro, because she would miss him so much, even though they had barely said more than a few words to each other throughout their entire lives.

Lupe arrived without her husband Quique, who had been arrested two days before, following an outburst in which he told the judge that he did not feel it was his responsibility to be a juror since he, as a homosexual, was not considered anyone's peer. He was just being a smartass, but it came as a total shock to his wife Lupe, who vowed she would rather let him rot in jail than post the bail necessary to win his freedom.

Toothless Coco arrived with a full set of choppers that everyone agreed were much too large—a secret contest was held to determine who looked more like a rabbit, Alberto with his big ears or Coco with his big teeth. He managed to cause quite a stir when he announced that he could not stay very long because his new wife, Sarah, the love of his life, whom he had married at city hall several months ago, was about to give birth any day now. No one had ever thought Coco would find himself a girlfriend, much less a wife.

Carlotta came very close to having a royal battle with Antonia when she was accused of bringing roaches into the house. It was not until it was discovered to be a raisin that had fallen from the *funche* that things quieted down in the kitchen. Nevertheless, she did manage to ruin the *funche* by over-stirring, turning it into corn meal mush. Antonia, of course, felt obligated to let her know.

Gloria, who vowed never to enter a church again, thus relinquishing her role as a godmother, received further condolences, along with many compliments on her gray hair, which seemed "so natural, unlike the color she used to wear," which irked Carlotta, who still looked very much like an eggplant.

Father O'Connor, who showed up for a little platter and a little cheer, brought a little bit of religion into the festivities as he

admiringly noted the blessing everyone gave to the food, not realizing that the waves of the hands were due to the tear in the
screen door which allowed an occasional fly to crash the party. It
was much too late for anyone to warn him later, as they tried to
do through their full mouths, when he sat down squarely on a full
box of opened chocolates and smashed them to bits. It took a
great deal of respect for no one to laugh as he was ushered toward
the bathroom with caramels and cherries dangling from his back-
side.

Once he felt presentable again, the honorable reverend
blessed Milagros one last time and departed. The festivities continued. El Bobo, who had told some very funny jokes, was forced
into silence by Coco, who ate one shrimp with hot sauce too
many and broke out in hives and a swollen tongue. It was a great
relief for all to find out that he hadn't swallowed his new teeth,
which they all agreed would have killed him.

The two *doñas*, Antonia and Esperanza, managed to avoid
each other for most of the party, but they were finally coerced by
their children into sitting next to each other for some fifteen minutes. Despite Antonia's apprehension and Esperanza's discomfort, together, they gushed over their mutual granddaughter,
whom they foresaw as a future belle of the ball. After all, didn't
she take after both sides of the family?

The men balked at having to dance instead of being allowed
to play poker on such a holy day, and they took their revenge out
on their wives by cutting in and dancing with each other. Lupe
had to be assured by everyone that they were just being buffoons
and had no intention of making fun of her situation. They begged
her to find it in her heart to pay the bail and have Quique
released, if only to kill him afterwards.

Everyone agreed by the end of the evening that it was a great
christening, considering there were no major fights or arguments
or other problems.

The next morning, coffee was served to Armando, the town drunk, who was found asleep on the front porch in his tattered gray suit and sneakers. He had wandered the previous evening, searching for the white house which had miraculously turned pale yellow. He had found his way to the one party that he finally missed.

# ～ TWENTY-SEVEN ～

No ONE COMPLAINED when Gloria sold the gas station to Anthony Ruggiero, the owner of the Italian pastry shop a few doors away. He and his four sons had expressed interest in purchasing it even before Pedro's death. Everyone in the family agreed that it would be best to be rid of the place that had caused them all such pain and anger.

Alberto went back to work at the *bodega*, which gave Antonia more time to spend with her granddaughter, who had become a little acrobat bent on balancing herself on her head in the playpen. The upside-down child had formed many bad habits in her short time on earth, such as finger painting with her own excrement and chewing on the furniture, but the most ominous was sucking on the wall as she stood in her crib. They would move the crib to the center of the room, only to find it back against the wall, never understanding how it got there.

Alberto and Pepitón were immediately ordered to cover the wall, which they did, with circus-motif wallpaper that only served to frighten the child out of her wits. At the first sight of the clowns Milagros screamed bloody murder, and once again the room had to be papered, this time with the choice being left up to the child. She was shown samples of various designs and took a liking to one that was covered with little pink pigs. Although they tried to coax her into something more subtle, the pink pigs won the day, and that was what she got.

When Milagros developed a terrible rash all over her body Antonia dismissed the notion that it was due to some type of voodoo. She and Amada rushed the child to the doctor's office. The pediatrician assured them it was just a form of poison ivy. Although uncomfortable, it would not cause any lasting problems. They were sent home with orders to rub calamine lotion on Milagros, which they did, but within hours the rash turned into terrible blisters. Amada called her mother for advice. Doña Esperanza expected the call of course, and was ready. When she arrived she went to work immediately. Over the objections of Antonia, Esperanza rubbed her special black salve on the child, and the blisters miraculously disappeared, leaving no trace of the awful affliction which would surely have disfigured Milagros for life.

"Voodoo, hoodoo!" was Antonia's response when Esperanza insisted they place a glass of clear water on top of the refrigerator to capture the many evil thoughts that were being directed toward the house and its occupants. Although not a superstitious person, Antonia finally did agree that things were not going as well as she would like and, after all, "What harm could a glass of water do?"

For some unknown reason, Antonia thought back to the previous week, when Mr. Feldman had announced that he was raising the rent of the *bodega*, which came as a shock to Pepitón, whose mention of the landlord's Jewish heritage brought a not-so-subtle response from Feldman that Pepitón could swim back to the island anytime he wished. Fortunately, Antonia had removed the pistol from the cigar box and hidden it in a sack of rice, and that averted what could have been a tragedy. After the shouting had died down, with Alberto acting as referee, the two men shook hands, agreeing they were both suffering from a great deal of stress. After all, neither of them had a prejudiced bone in his body. Obviously the entire conflict was over money and had absolutely nothing to do with voodoo of any sort, but Antonia did notice that the water in the glass filled up with bubbles instantly. Just as quickly, she assumed the change in its appearance was due to a change in the atmosphere.

"Voodoo, hoodoo!" was her same reaction when her daughter-in-law began to speak in a language that no one understood. Antonia attributed this strange behavior to the fact that the girl's mother was weird. Therefore, "Like mother, like daughter." It was only when a very large black crow flew in through the fireplace and stared Antonia directly in the eyes that she became a true believer.

As big a woman as she was, she was terrified of anything that had wings. Rather than chase the flying intruder toward the window, the crow chased *her* from room to room as she screamed at the top of her lungs. When Pepitón came home from work he found her sitting out front in her dressing gown. He scolded her for her cowardice and ridiculed her for doing battle with a bird, which turned out to be much smaller than she had imagined it to be. What in her mind was the size of an eagle was in his eyes the size of a sparrow. An argument ensued in which he finally acquiesced that it was, indeed, large enough to carry someone such as herself off into the heavens. From that day on, the flue in the fireplace remained closed, and screens were mended on the windows and doors so that not even a fruit fly could trespass.

It was shortly after that fiasco that the seizures began. Antonia and Amada were tying up the *pasteles* they had been preparing for hours and were about to place them into the pots of boiling water, when Antonia noticed Amada's body begin to tremble, slightly at first, and then suddenly with a great deal of ferocity. It was all she could do to deflect the pot away from Amada as it crashed onto the kitchen floor, spraying its contents away from both of the women and averting serious harm to either of them.

That seizure was followed by another and another, causing Amada to be carried to bed because her legs could not hold up the weight of her body. Amada tried to explain the episodes away, but when it became clear that they were not due to her being tired, she was taken to a specialist after none of the general practitioners could find a reason for these fits. She had X-rays taken and was given test after test, including a painful spinal tap. When the results were non-conclusive she was finally diagnosed as having hysterical paralysis, probably due to the fact that she was once again pregnant.

Amada was growing more and more despondent, and Alberto was urged to be more attentive to her, which he already was. He had broken up with Sarah after Pedro died. He realized how much he did love his wife and no longer stayed out all hours. He had made it a weekly ritual to bring her flowers and candy, trying to atone for his stupidity. He had become the good husband that he was initially expected to be and doted over the two most important ladies in his life. The more attentive he was to his wife and daughter, though, the worse the seizures became. Amada had constant thoughts of suicide, and was watched at all times by at least one member of the family for fear that she would make good on her threats.

Doña Esperanza, on the other hand, knew that someone had done a *trabajo* on her daughter and was "damned if she would let the miserable son of a bitch, whoever it may be, get away with it." She had Joaquín accompany her across the bridge to the wooded area beyond Hunts Point, where she picked *yerbabuena* from among the weeds that grew there. She came back and brewed a medicinal tea from the fresh mint. She also made a mixture of oil and Florida water mixed with other rare herbs and rubbed the warm, soothing liquid on her daughter's legs, which seemed to help only temporarily.

Praying for a miracle, Doña Esperanza forced her daughter to visit a home in Coney Island to see a statue of the Virgin Mary that was reported to cry real tears. They waited in line among the many believers until they stood before the statue and did, indeed, see tears flow from its eyes. Esperanza wiped one of the tears with her lace handkerchief and placed it in her purse. When she arrived home later that evening, she opened the handkerchief to discover that the tear drop had turned into a live, ugly worm. Repulsed, she folded the handkerchief, secured it in a box, tied it tightly and placed it next to the Infant of Prague, her daughter's saint, on the home altar.

Esperanza spent all night praying before that altar to every saint and spirit that was good, beseeching them to use their powers to intervene on her daughter's behalf. The following day, when she opened the box, the worm had disappeared and so had Amada's seizures.

# ~ TWENTY-EIGHT ~

CARLOTTA, who was not to be thwarted by Gloria's mourning period, took matters into her own hands and insisted that Antonia once again return to the routine of Sunday dinners, if only for Gloria's sake. It was unnatural for Gloria, Carlotta insisted, to spend most of the week locked in her apartment watching soap operas, while her weekends were spent at Woodlawn Cemetery, picking up the dried leaves and dead branches that accumulated around Pedro's grave. Seemingly the grave was given no care, despite her many trips to the office to complain. After Carlotta's relentless phone calls and daily visits to Gloria's apartment, Gloria reluctantly gave in and agreed to once again partake of Sunday dinner with the family. Gloria was almost instantly brought back to life.

~ ~ ~

One Sunday, at Carlotta's insistence, the men offered to teach Gloria the fundamentals of driving, for Pedro's new Ford needed to be driven or it would eventually have to be junked. Pepitón's method of teaching was a mixture of expletives followed by apologies. Alberto insisted that she not be so shy with the gas pedal, because his middle finger had grown weary from the many gestures he gave the impatient drivers who trailed behind them at

ten miles per hour. Surprisingly, it was Che who gave the best les-
sons. His inability to hear the honking of horns allowed him to
concentrate on what he was doing, which was, as he put it, "easy
as cake." When it came time for Gloria's road test, all three men
were on hand to give her moral support and to make sure that the
inspector did not treat her unfairly, as they did most women drivers. After crossing their fingers while watching her drive away,
they each fingered the envelopes of cash in their pockets, just in
case she ran a stop sign or hit the curb while parking. When she
passed the test on her own the envelopes were instead used to treat
her to a celebratory drink at Clark's Bar, where the patrons, who
at first showed their disapproval at the intrusion on their macho
privacy by turning their backs, quickly joined in the congratula-
tions when drinks were ordered for the house.

~ ~ ~

It was not long before Carlotta insisted that she and Gloria
seek employment, "Just for pin money, of course." Carlotta had
recently lost her job at The Velvet Twist, even though she insisted
to her employer that she had been late only fourteen times—not
fifteen. Gloria no doubt would once again have to color her hair,
for everyone knew that in order to gain employment one had to
at least *look* young. Reluctantly, Gloria agreed, but rather than
eggplant she chose an auburn, which made her appear quite
attractive. Following that, both women searched for and finally
found jobs at the five-and-dime on Southern Boulevard.

Although they worked in different departments, Gloria in
Notions and Carlotta in Cosmetics, the two would meet at the
lunch counter every day, where they ate and talked about everyone's foibles but their own; the girl in Toys had a terrible deodor-
ant problem, the manager must have had the clap—for he was
always scratching his privates. . . . They especially wagged their
tongues about the woman in Lingerie, who Gloria was sure was

a he-she, because one day she noticed from the bottom of the adjacent bathroom stall that her very large feet *faced* the toilet bowl when she urinated. Not that it mattered, they agreed, for every family, theirs included, had at least one member who was sexually different. It was only when Antonia was mentioned soon after that they lost control and were asked to leave the lunch counter after annoying the other customers with their raucous laughter.

Payday was a total disappointment to Carlotta. After deductions for payroll tax and social security, along with further deductions for the large lunches she had put on her tab, she was terribly insulted by her meager paycheck. She decided she could not afford to work there any longer and quit, shaming Gloria into doing the same.

$$\sim \, \sim \, \sim$$

Following their very short stint as salesgirls, Carlotta thought it would be wise for them to enroll in classes, which would give them a chance at something more lucrative, perhaps enabling them to go into business on their own. And so it was that they enrolled in The Wilfred Academy of Beauty with the intention of one day opening their own beauty salon. They took days to decide on a name for their future establishment, finally agreeing on "The CurliCute," after cutting it down from the "Curlicuticle." CurliCute was, they felt, more descriptive of a place that covered both hair and nails at the same time. Graduation from the academy, however, never took place. One day, after inspecting what could only be described as the largest beehive hairdo in history, a beehive that Gloria had created for an unpleasant blue-haired woman, Carlotta went into an uncontrollable fit of laughter, which quickly turned into a chain reaction. The more incensed the woman became, the louder the laughter until Carlotta, after wetting her pants, went screeching from the room, with Gloria giving chase. They were both told never to return.

As they drove home on the Bronx River Parkway, past the cemetery, Carlotta interrupted Gloria's silent prayer by announcing it was time they both take a vacation. And in less than a month, the family was at the docks of the Grace Line, waving their *bon voyage* to the two "vagabonds," as Antonia had taken to calling them, when they sailed off to Venezuela.

"Why Venezuela?" was the question everyone asked, when they finally got around to asking Gloria and Carlotta.

The answer was the old, familiar line, "Because we have family there." This only led to, "What family are you talking about?" That was followed by, "Don't you remember when Lola came to visit when we were kids and she told us about a cousin Elliot and the family that came from England and settled in Venezuela?" Of course, they didn't, but that didn't matter because that brought up: "Amílcar, who fought in the Venezuelan army (and flew a plane by the way)," who was related to Carlotta, not Gloria who had mentioned Elliot to begin with, and *they* were not related at all... at least they did not think they were, although when they had dyed their hair, they did look like sisters. And then there was the matter of Chicha, who resembled absolutely no one in anyone's family that they could think of. She could have been Venezuelan, or was that Mercedes? They really didn't know much about Mercedes, so they left it at that.

It was too late to figure it out since they had already gotten in touch with this Elliot character, who said he would be happy to have them stay with him and his mother during their time in Caracas, and like that, the plans were set in motion. Who cared if they knew each other or not? They would still have a great time and be treated like royalty, because they were only staying a short time. And the Venezuelans for their part felt it would be nice to be visited by Americans. They always knew they had family in the U.S. of A., so *why not* Gloria and Carlotta?

~ ~ ~

It was during this time away from his wife that Che was arrested for indecent exposure on the I. R. T. He, as a creature of habit, had dropped his car off for a tune-up at his brother's old garage, which was now named after the Ruggiero Brothers, forgetting for a moment that his brother would not be there to run out to meet him. Embarrassed by his thoughtlessness, he left the car there after exchanging his keys for a voucher, which offered a free cannoli at the bakery. He then took the subway to Longwood Avenue to visit Pepitón's *bodega*.

As he exited the train a woman who had been staring at him throughout the ride called him over. When Che ignored her, either because he did not hear her or because he was not interested, he was accosted by her partner, who was dressed in uniform. The cop immediately handcuffed Che's hands behind his back. Only when the woman pulled a badge from her purse and pointed to his open fly did he remember that Carlotta had placed these particular trousers with the clothes that were to be mended. He was both shocked and embarrassed because he was not allowed to zip his pants and was forced to walk through the crowd with his fly open while strangers jeered at him and called him a pervert.

When Pepitón arrived at the Simpson St. station to get his brother, it took everything in his power not to kill the guardians of the law, who insisted the blackened eyes and the blood that covered his brother's broken nose was due to his falling down the stairs after resisting arrest, and not his lack of cooperation when they asked him the usual questions. It was when this giant of a man broke down in tears before them, explaining that his brother was deaf, that they shuffled their feet with a tinge of embarrassment and allowed Pepitón to take his brother home. But never once did they admit any culpability on their part while insisting they were letting him off easy by tearing up the arrest papers, providing he kept his nose clean and his pants zipped from then on.

This emasculating episode, which left yet another scar on both men, did merit God's attention. After being treated for his wounds at Hunt's Point Hospital by the young, amiable Dr. García, it was made clear to Che that his deafness was not due to his trumpet playing days, as they all had surmised, but rather a great accumulation of wax, which could be drained, enabling him to hear again.

A week later when Che put the shiny brass trumpet to his trembling lips, the same horn that he had polished every day of his life, his throat choked with pain as he once again heard the beautiful music that he loved, and he wept like a small child. He wept for the time that he had wasted in silence, but most of all he wept for his brother Pedro, whom he had forgotten for a moment and who would never again be there to encourage him to play the music he loved with all his heart. He had not shed a tear at the wake, nor at the cemetery, and as he put the trumpet back into its case and placed it under his bed, he apologized to his brother and vowed never to play it again.

# ∼ Twenty-nine ∼

ILIANA'S BIRTH came without much fanfare. Alberto and Amada arrived at Lincoln Hospital at eight o'clock in the morning, and by eight-thirty Iliana was born. Dr. Mound, who had prepared himself for another possible hairy ape was astonished to find that this newborn, unlike her sister, was totally bald and held a strong resemblance to Alfred Hitchcock.

Everyone agreed that she was a beautiful child, including Alberto, who although wishing for a son, could not help but marvel at the child who had his mother's hazel eyes and Pepitón's bald head. Although Doña Esperanza could not argue with his assessment of the lack of hair, she was quick to point out that both *her* mother and father had hazel eyes, as did Amada when she was born. If Alberto had taken the time to look, he would have noticed that Amada's eyes still changed color when they were exposed to the sunlight, which was rare because she never went out much anymore, not to mention the fact that they had remained violet ever since she went to Puerto Rico.

It was only Milagros, who took an instant dislike to her baby sister, who caused concern. Screaming at the top of her lungs and covering her eyes with her hands, she did not allow anyone to console her or shut her up. It took very little time to realize that Milagros, who was now toddling, could not be trusted near Iliana. She made it quite clear that this little intruder did not merit the attention everyone was bestowing on her and was therefore not welcome in her room, her parent's room or any other part of the house for that matter.

Iliana's bassinet, which had originally belonged to Milagros, was moved to Amada and Alberto's bedroom when the toddler was found sucking on the baby's arm in an effort to bite it off with the few baby teeth in her mouth. There was very little sleep to be had from that day on, because Milagros had somehow learned to climb out of her crib. She was found on more than one occasion standing over Iliana in the middle of the night. She would pinch her and poke at her, at times taking aim at her eyes. All attempts to deter her from misbehaving were futile. She would scream for hours on end, disturbing the entire household, as well other households in the vicinity.

Antonia, who never believed in "spare the rod *caca*," waited for her chance to be alone with Milagros in order to teach her the proper way for a young lady to behave. When Alberto and Amada finally agreed that a quiet walk around the block together would be a nice change of pace for them, Antonia jumped at the chance to teach the little monster a thing or two. What she hadn't counted on when she smacked the little girl on the behind for terrorizing her sister was Milagros' ability to hold her breath, turn blue and faint. Antonia's shrieks could be heard throughout the neighborhood. She was certain she had killed her granddaughter, alarming Alberto and Amada into a hasty retreat back into the house and an immediate beeline to the emergency room.

Milagros regained her breath and her color, but she let it be known that any attempt to chastise her would only precipitate more of the same blue action. Even the kindly Dr. Mound was treated to a dose of her temper when he attempted to give her a vaccination. She again turned on the blue, this time in his office.

It was only after speaking with a specialist in child psychology that Amada was told to simply allow the child her tantrum, making certain that when she fainted there was nothing she would fall against that could cause her any harm. Once Milagros realized that no one seemed to care about her blue periods, she no longer held her breath. In the meantime, everyone slept a little better, and things went back to normal, or as normal as possible.

After about a week or two, the spelling game began. Both Amada and Alberto learned that their precocious Milagros could understand everything that was said about her, so they had to spell everything in order for her not to have a tantrum. This meant spelling out words they hoped she would not understand. It took a toll on them because Milagros understood both Spanish and English. Neither Antonia nor Pepitón believed she could be that smart until Antonia had the effrontery to say, "*No me vengan con esa mierda sicológica*," to which Milagros replied, "What psychological *caca*, Grandma?"Antonia quickly joined the others in learning to spell.

It took a while, but eventually things calmed down. Milagros began to take a liking to her sister and found it was easier to be nice than obstinate and mean. She could achieve her desired results by just getting along.

# ～ Thirty ～

WHEN CARLOTTA AND GLORIA disembarked it was Che and Pepitón who met them at the dock. Carlotta, unlike most of the other passengers, came down the stairs looking as if she had just arrived from a trip to the Bahamas. She was wearing bright, flowery tourist garb and a large straw hat that all but covered her eggplant hair, which had turned orange in the Venezuelan sun.

Much to the annoyance of her fellow passengers, tripping over her on their way out, Carlotta immediately got on her knees, kissed the ground and blessed the Statue of Liberty and the Frenchman who had given her to America. Che, although glad to see her, was not too thrilled to hear her voice, which he had forgotten was so shrill and nasal, as she broke into an impromptu version of The Star Spangled Banner to the delight of the American tourists and the dirty looks of the Venezuelans, who were glad to be rid of this all-too-patriotic pest.

Carlotta was thrilled to learn that Che had regained his hearing, but this joy was tempered by the fact that she could no longer speak about him in the third person anymore. This was a habit she had developed throughout the long quiet years, and she would have to be careful in the future, now that his vocabulary no longer consisted solely of "*¿Qué?*"

Both brothers were slightly annoyed when Gloria insisted they meet Elliot, a tall, mustachioed, dark-haired Venezuelan who had accompanied them on their journey home. They were further annoyed, and yet grateful, when they learned he had been responsible for rescuing them from possible imprisonment in Caracas. Carlotta, who felt it was her right as an American citizen to criticize anything that she found criticizable, had expressed her ideas on democracy to two armed presidential guards who did not share her view. It was only because of his intercession that both women were not detained, and they had spent many an evening following the cursing of the guards touring Caracas with Elliot as their guide. Gloria found Venezuela breathtaking, while Carlotta spent most of her vacation complaining about the inability to say and do as she pleased.

"You have no idea what it's like to not be able to say exactly what you feel *when* you feel it. You have to just shut up like a child if something bothers you, even if it means getting an ulcer, which I'm sure I have, because I didn't bring my Maalox with me and I had to keep quiet about everything, which is something I can't do when I'm annoyed. You know that as well as anyone, and yet, there I was, shutting my mouth at every turn. It was impossible to have fun and shut up at the same time, if you know what I mean. Awful, just awful, that's all I can say—and yet it was a wonderful trip. If I could only have spoke my mind like I do in America, the country that I love with all of my heart and appreciate now more than ever. Do you know what I mean?"

The brothers nodded their heads in agreement, not understanding a word she had said as they exchanged formal greetings with the handsome Elliot. They made an extra effort not to prejudge his all-too-correct manner, which they took to be slimy, all the while noticing that Gloria seemed much too familiar with him, something they would criticize her for later, during the car ride home. It was only when Elliot's mother, Doña Josefina, nudged her son from behind, advising him that they were in a hurry to get their luggage, that they noticed this dumpy little woman under a cowboy hat with a large cigar dangling from her lips. They made an immediate U-turn in order to avoid laughing directly in her face. Once able to compose themselves, they said their "Mucho gustos" and their "Adioses," exchanging addresses and courtesies in between. They then hurried to get the "girls'" luggage, because Antonia was alone minding the store and expected Pepitón to be back as soon as possible.

Carlotta spent the entire ride home criticizing Venezuela, while Gloria did nothing but speak of Elliot and what a gentleman he was. He had gone out of his way to show them how beautiful the country was, and if Carlotta would have given it a chance, she might have had a good time too. Carlotta disagreed one hundred percent and was glad to be back, "in the home of the brave and the land of the free," she sang, mangling the national anthem. The last part was sung in a way that made Che contemplate suicide. Pepitón could not have cared less as he sped along the Major Deegan Expressway, looking forward to finally parking the car and not having to listen to either woman.

*Am I glad I'm married to Antonia*, he mused, thinking how wonderful it would be if Venezuela had detained them for another month. But that would have been too much to ask. The Lord was busy with other things, so why bother him with little problems?

Meanwhile, Antonia, who had insisted she was perfectly capable of tending the store by herself, urged Alberto to stay home to help Amada with their two daughters. Amada had been looking ill lately. There was something ghostly about her daughter-in-law's demeanor, which made Antonia shiver, feeling darkness follow the girl from room to room. This was not the young woman she had tortured during her first year of marriage and whom she had since grown to love as a daughter; this was a tormented soul, one who spent her every waking moment in a struggle to retain her sanity.

When Antonia heard the little bell which hung over the *bodega* door, she was surprised to see a very toothy Coco enter, followed by his little son, Jorge, who was nicknamed Cucho and who was approximately the same age as Milagros. She could feel her heart pounding in her throat as she looked upon this little boy, who held no resemblance to Coco, but rather was the spitting image of her own son. The resemblance was uncanny considering the fact that Coco was such a distant relative who resembled no one in the immediate family. It became very clear after the boy's mother, Sarah, made her entrance a few moments later, what exactly had transpired. Antonia's legs gave out from under her as she dropped to the floor in a dead faint.

## ∼Thirty-one ∼

COCO FELT LITTLE JORGE'S FINGERS grip his hand tightly as he heard the hushed voices rise in their hostility from the back room of the *bodega*. Antonia, once revived, had given a few lame excuses for her sudden collapse. Now, she and Sarah had secluded themselves from the others, after having posted the "CLOSED" sign on the door of the shop. Although Coco was far from being a genius, he was even farther from being a moron, which is precisely what he felt like at that very moment. What had begun as a proud day on which he was to introduce his beautiful son to some of his relatives, who had all, for one reason or another, sent their regrets at not being able to attend the boy's baptism, had become the day on which the secret that suddenly drove him to the depths of despair was unearthed.

He was grateful for the jingling distraction of the Good Humor truck that stopped a few doors away, and he quickly whisked his little boy out of the store, stopping to buy him an ice cream as they made their way home in silence. He had never questioned. He had never counted. He had assumed, as he always did when a bit of good fortune came his way, that God was finally giving him a break in life.

Coco and his brothers and sisters had never been fully accepted by the family. He never understood why, but attributed their arms-length attitude to the fact that no one had cared for his mother, who was quite dark and whose features were not entirely Hispanic, as he had heard mentioned more than once in his lifetime. It also had been said that she enjoyed her drinks just a little too much for their liking. They had tolerated her, for the sake of his father, but after she had taken up with another man and abandoned them all to run off with him, neither she nor her children were looked upon as *real* family again. From then on, they were only invited to the occasional festivities, where everyone became family again until the next occasion.

Coco's father, wallowing in self-pity, soon became a bitter alcoholic. When he was not abusing the children, he disappeared for days, leaving them to beg in the streets for food from strangers. After a few prolonged, but futile, detoxifying visits to Pilgrim State Hospital, he finally took his own life.

The children were all shipped off by the authorities to spend their youth at a Catholic home upstate, visited only occasionally by the so-called family. At first, they were all ready to adopt the kids, one in each home, but the church insisted that they all stay together, and no one could afford that. After a long battle with the church, which went nowhere, they finally just gave up. It was there that Coco came to both fear and despise nuns and the Christianity they practiced in words only. It was there that he learned to talk and act like the street kid that so many of the other children there were. And it was there that he lost his teeth, when one of the bigger boys who had always bullied him purposely elbowed him as he placed a bottle of Coca-Cola to his lips. One by one, as the children graduated, they were sent out into the world, never quite ready to face the traumas it held for them, and one by one they failed, until only Coco was left behind to represent them on this earth.

After a short stint in the Army he eventually went to work for Sears, stocking shelves and taking inventory. He was, much to the surprise of his coworkers, great at selling oriental rugs. He

was good at talking up the merchandise because he really
believed it was beautiful. He took great pains to show the delicate
weaving that had been done and the colors that *seemed* faded, yet
stood out to anyone who understood the rug business. In other
words, he could bullshit better than the other salesmen, and he
enjoyed his status there.

He remembered that was how he met Sarah—trying to sell
her and an older fellow a rug, which by the way was the best of
the lot. The old guy had pretended he knew what he was talking
about but really knew nothing. He let the man show off and then
zeroed in for the sale when he let him know that the Shah of Iran
had the identical rug in his palace. How he knew this remained a
closely guarded secret, but really he had seen it on "60 Minutes"
or some other TV show a long time ago.

Sarah was impressed with how much he knew, and, little by
little, the old man became older and pallid almost to the point of
disappearing, while Coco boasted about his travels and other
things he made up. By the time the rug was bought he had made
a date with Sarah for coffee. The rest was history.

As Coco and little Jorge climbed the stairs to their apartment,
they met Doña Marina, the kindly neighbor who had no children
of her own, but was the surrogate mother to all of the children in
the neighborhood. She found nothing strange in Coco's request
that she watch little Jorge for a while, because her home was
brimming with others who had come to partake of the cookies
she baked and the stories she would read to them. As he used his
monogrammed handkerchief to wipe the remains of the chocolate
ice cream from Jorge's face, he elicited a smile from the very
sleepy boy and kissed him goodbye.

Once inside his apartment Coco was driven by rage; the animal within him overtook any presence of mind that might have

stopped him. He blew out the candle in the glass of seven colors that stood before their wedding photo. He broke the glass in the bathtub. Its contents spilled over the enamel and down the drain. He scrubbed away the blue exes that Sarah had chalked on the doors and gathered the rock, the piece of wood and all of the other inanimate objects that his wife had treated with a certain reverence and threw them out of the living room window and into the alley. He ripped the goatskin from the wall and stuffed it into a shopping bag, along with the coconut which he had seen rolled across the floor *so* many times, and which had until this moment lain in a corner near the entrance of the apartment. As he scanned the room for anything of importance he may have missed, he could feel the string of tiny beads that Sarah had placed around his neck for good luck tighten, break and scatter all over the linoleum. Scooping up as many as he could gather into the bag, he tossed it out of the window. He, who had known so little joy in life, followed the bag out the window, down into the dirty alleyway below, and he was ultimately released from his pain.

# ∼ THIRTY-TWO ∼

COCO'S WAKE, which was held at the Ortiz Funeral Home on Prospect Avenue, drew the usual crowd, minus a few out-of-state relatives who could not attend due to the fact that, much to their consternation, the wake was only to be a one-day affair. They had been told that unless they were willing to fork over the dollars required to prolong the event, this was one occasion they would have to miss, which is precisely what they did, as was noted by the few names missing in the register at the back of the room.

Although the majority of the flowers that arrived were those in baskets and not the elaborate crosses and wreaths that were sent for the more important deceased, one large, bleeding heart made up entirely of roses was present, thanks to Pepitón and Antonia, who agreed it was only right that he receive at least one decent arrangement, no matter the cost. The fact that they had obtained a discount from the florist on Westchester Avenue in exchange for the business they pushed his way from their customers at the *bodega* never entered the conversation, at least not within hearing distance of anyone attending the wake. Every new arrival of flowers brought on a not-so-inconspicuous move to read the cards that accompanied them.

On top of the closed casket that held Coco's remains was a photograph that had been the object of a great search through family photo albums for a current, yet decent, photo of the deceased. The nicest picture of him, where he was not exposing a toothless smile, was a closed-mouthed photo taken at Orchard Beach, but the fact that he was clad in only a bathing suit immediately disqualified that photo, even after someone suggested cutting out just the head and enlarging it, which was frowned upon as even more tasteless than just using the photo itself. In the one snapshot of him that was taken at Milagros' christening he bore a remarkable resemblance to a donkey as he proudly dazzled everyone with his new teeth. Aside from the fact that they felt it would bring bad luck to Milagros, they worried that everyone might laugh at him, and this was not a laughing matter. They finally decided on the wedding photograph that was found in his apartment. They cut Sarah out of the picture completely. She had disappeared with the couple's son Jorge before anyone in the family, except for Antonia, ever set eyes on him. It was scandalous that she had not made an appearance or allowed Jorge to say goodbye to his beloved father.

It was a crying shame that the family had to learn of Coco's death from two police officers. They showed up at the *bodega* after being told by Coco's neighbors that his family owned a grocery store somewhere in the neighborhood. That Sarah had taken off, no matter the circumstances surrounding his death, and had not had the decency to tell anyone what had happened made her the pariah of the family, most of whom had no idea who she was, nor did they care to know.

It was Pepitón and Alberto who went, first to Lincoln Hospital and then to the morgue in Manhattan, to identify the remains after the police had confronted them with the terrible news. It was these same two who later searched his apartment, where they found Coco's yellow-striped, cardboard suitcase whose contents included a few belongings, among them his honorable discharge from the Army and a Bible that he had taken from a motel room. Stuck in the Bible's pages was a faded picture of his parents and siblings before their world had been turned upside-down. They also found the dental bridge that had been made for him in the service, wrapped neatly in a tissue, which he rarely wore because of the considerable pain it bore him. In the hall closet they found only the familiar gray suit he wore to all functions and which he would now wear to the last family function he would be a part of.

The fact that he had served in the Army guaranteed him a plot in Long Island National Cemetery and $250. The family used the $250 dollars to help pay for the wake and for the rest of the arrangements which were, if not grand, sufficient enough to soothe their consciences. The church, with its anti-suicide restrictions, had refused a Mass for him, even though a substantial donation in his name had been placed in an envelope in the poor box. However, Father O'Connor did agree, as a favor, to lead the prayers at the wake, which he said in English while many of the attendees repeated them in Spanish.

Talk of Sarah, and whether she would have the audacity to show her face, dominated the conversation, only to be quickly replaced by talk about Gloria, who everyone assumed was still much too devastated by the death of Pedro to be required to go through this emotional ritual. When she shockingly showed up, accompanied by Elliot, the mustachioed Venezuelan, nothing was said to her face, but there was a buzz of scandal throughout the wake. Gloria did interrupt a group of ladies in the restroom who were arguing her case, pro and con, and she let them know, from inside one of the few stalls, that it was, in reality, "None of their damned business."

No one, with the exception of Antonia, could imagine what had happened to drive Coco to such an act. It was only after persuading themselves that, "He was never really all-there mentally," that the funereal fiction began: "He was a man of impeccable taste."

"He was tasteless, but sweet."

"He was so handsome."

"He looked like a rabbit, the poor thing."

"He had a smile for everyone."

"He was the most boring person I ever knew, although the kindest, for one should never speak ill of the dead, especially not in the confines of a funeral home, where many unhappy spirits lurk."

Everyone had a story to tell about Coco, and everyone was eager to tell it. No matter that it was really his brother who had replaced the sugar with salt on April Fool's Day; he was remembered for the dastardly act for which his grandmother became sick and had to be rushed to Emergency for palpitations, all the while being reassured that no one was out to poison her—especially not her deceased husband's first wife. It was the terrible case of chicken pox that he had contracted as a child that left him pockmarked, or was that Chicha's son with all of the holes in his face? He definitely was the one who was inhabited by spirits, "'cause didn't he sing the Ave María in a woman's voice when he was only three years old?" And wasn't he the one who almost drowned in a Crotona swimming pool when that group of Italian boys tossed him in the deep water and he didn't know how to swim? He had developed a hearing problem from that day on, or were they confusing him with Che? One by one, they recalled stories of the dearly departed, stories that were occasionally interrupted by a wail of remembrance or a loudly blown nose.

Coco's funeral would have ended without incident had it not been for a dark-skinned old woman who seemingly appeared out of nowhere and knelt to say a prayer in front of the coffin. No one was certain, but the whispers made it clear that everyone thought she bore much too striking a resemblance—although she was much older—to the woman who had abandoned her family and children so many years ago.

She had not signed the register, so Carlotta's quick dash, at Antonia's urging, to read the names in the book did her no good. No one could be certain as thoughts of tossing "Coco's whore mother" out, if indeed it was the tramp, raced through everyone's minds, along with the possibility that they might be mistaken. They did not want to make total asses of themselves. After all, how would she have known, unless she had read the obituary pages in the *Daily News,* that her son had died? Rather than cause a disturbance which they felt would be inappropriate, they instead quietly simmered in corners until she rose and walked away. No one approached her, nor did she attempt to approach anyone there. It was only after her disappearance that most of the men folk, who avoided confrontation like the plague, breathed loud sighs of relief.

Hours later, as they stood at the gravesite, more than one set of eyes searched the area for this stranger. Most attendees had come to the conclusion that she had indeed been Coco's mother. The women there would have liked nothing better than to kick her into the open hole which stood waiting for her son. Fortunately for her, they never saw her again. It should be noted that Chicha, who had made a fool of herself at Pedro's funeral by threatening to jump into his grave, sensing the mood of the crowd, wisely kept her composure as well as her distance at this particular funeral.

## ∽ THIRTY-THREE ∽

GLORIA SHOVED ELLIOT down everyone's throats—at least that's how they perceived it. It began with short drop-by visits to Che and Carlotta, the latter showing her disapproval by not putting out the usual cheese and crackers topped with green olives she offered to everyone who set foot in her apartment. This did not go unnoticed by Gloria, who vowed silently to never offer Carlotta a glass of water, even if she were stranded on a desert island and forced to drink coconut milk for the rest of her life.

The fact that Carlotta, who made it her business to always be prepared, had been caught with her hair in rollers, or having just taken a shower and not ready to receive guests, did not matter to Gloria. She just knew that there was no place for rudeness where Elliot was concerned, no matter what the excuse was.

The parading of Elliot continued into Alberto and Amada's home, with the pretext of wanting to see the "two beautiful little girls," one of whom would have been her godchild, had the devil not intervened, and the other adorable, bald baby who would *soon* be her godchild if she had anything to say about it. And say she did, over and over and over again until the agreement was ratified. Iliana, who had not yet uttered her first words, had very little say in the matter, other than to spit up her meals whenever Gloria took her in her arms and played "goo-goo" with her.

The shoving ultimately escalated into the unavoidable, although self-imposed invitation to Sunday dinner at Antonia's and Pepitón's house. The fact that the couple were accompanied by Elliot's very strange mother, who barely spoke while smoking her cigars in a corner chair, did not sit well with Antonia, who scurried to add an extra place setting to the table, as well as to replace the candy dish which she was certain would be confused with an ashtray. Antonia would insist for days afterward that the foul odor from the putrid cigars would never come out of the drapes.

Elliot, who had no ill intentions, was instantly disliked because of his annoying tendency to belittle everyone and everything. Exactly who he was also perplexed the family. Just how rich he and his family were was still in question, for no one seemed to be able to elicit any consistent answers about either his background or the source of his wealth. Yes, he had a home that came very close to being a mansion, but was it in Maracaibo, as he said in one breath—or Caracas, as he said in another. And yes, his money had come from oil, yet mining and banking had entered the conversation at one point or another. His mother, who sat silently adoring him, only added to the confusion as she nodded in assent to all of his tales. The one thing they all agreed on, in silence of course, was that he was perfect for Gloria, who always held an air of snobbery and who had never made sense to them either. Many a conversation was peppered with the fact that if it ever rained, Gloria would drown because her nose was always up in the air.

They did, however, enjoy Elliot's tales of European travels, whether true or not, because they had always dreamed of visiting the continent. Alberto especially liked hearing first-hand accounts of places he had only read about, and he appeared agitated by the fact that his youth seemed to be slipping away from him. Alberto had devoured books as a child, hoping one day to visit the many places he had read about and not be limited to a life in the Bronx. He had wanted to be *somebody*, but just who that somebody was always eluded him.

Although the men were fascinated by the stories Elliot told, it was Antonia who cut short the conversation, when his recollections of Amsterdam came much too close to pornography for her liking and therefore was not appropriate in mixed company.

Exactly what it was that bothered them about Elliot they could never pinpoint, but bother them he did. Maybe it was a Venezuelan thing, but there was a snobbishness about him that they couldn't put their finger on. They were irked by the way he folded his handkerchief, the way he blew his nose, the way he cracked his knuckles and the way he boasted about everything, no matter that it meant absolutely nothing to them.

Elliot's whole being seemed incongruous. For instance, there was no doubt in their minds that the huge medallion of the Virgin that graced Elliot's chest was genuine platinum, but the fact that he counted every chip when he played poker, squirreling away the dollar bills he won into his socks, made him appear to need every dime he got his hands on. At one point, as he chortled with glee while raking in a hand after an obvious bluff, Che was forced to bite his tongue rather than blurt out the fact that if he needed money that badly there were pawn shops that would be willing to exchange his ridiculous medallion for cash.

All of these flaws seemed insignificant in comparison to the *faux pas* he made one Sunday afternoon that could have cost him his life. He said that Fidel Castro was not really an evil man and had only turned to Russia because the United States had abandoned him. Pepitón and Che jumped to their feet, ready to toss him out on his ear with his doting mother behind him. They roared like lions and assailed him as a Communist. Gloria, who tried to intervene, was attacked as an "idiot for bringing a Communist-Marxist-Leninist into our midst." There was no stopping either brother in their tirade and they declared that Elliot's stupidity could get him shot.

"Not evil? *Not evil?!!*" Che sputtered, as if the words would choke him if he didn't spit them out. "What, are you stupid? Are you crazy? And what about the missiles? The missiles he was going to blow us all up with? *That* wasn't evil?"

"I just meant . . . " Elliot tried to clarify.

"And our homes?" Pepitón shouted in his other ear. "Are we supposed to thank him for taking everything away from us? I guess you think we should say "Thank you, Fidel," and forget about it. What the hell is wrong with you?"

"And what about the writers and the journalists that he put in jail?" Everyone was screaming now. "And the homosexuals that he imprisoned? Do you think that was right, too?"

It was bad enough that he had excused the dictator's evil deeds, the very same leader who had ruined their homeland, but to follow in the same breath with a slight against the United States, the greatest country on this earth (after Cuba), was unforgivable. He was apprised of the fact that he should kiss the ground he walked on, or else take the first available plane back to Caracas or Maracaibo or Timbuktu for all they cared.

Everyone was on their feet now, trying to avoid or provoke a fight. The women tried to remind them that there were little babies present and they were acting like buffoons, scaring the children. Milagros had begun to scream loudly, first wetting her pants and then going into her blue faint. Iliana, on the other hand, seemed to take the great commotion in stride. It was only when the brothers had settled down that Elliot apologized and said he had been misunderstood.

Just then, in the newborn silence, they heard the first word ever uttered by Iliana. The baby, who lay giggling in her bassinet, pointed to the unseen and repeated over and over again: "Coco!"

## ⌁ Thirty-four ⌁

From the moment of Iliana's revelation people saw Coco everywhere, even as far away as Los Angeles, where a vacationing Mecha, swore on the life of her mother that he appeared to her, stark naked, at a Holiday Inn swimming pool. This sighting was dismissed as the ranting of a woman who had undoubtedly enjoyed one peach brandy too many.

Other appearances by Coco, however, were impossible to discredit, especially when it was the non-believers who recounted their experiences. Doña Antonia saw Coco in her kitchen while she was beating the egg whites for her famous meringues. She quickly whisked him out of her kitchen with a broom, adding that he was not welcome there; because he was *dead*, she defiantly reminded him. "Go to the place where dead people go, wherever that may be, and stop frightening people."

Pepitón never saw Coco, but was present on more than one occasion when his wife would begin shouting at the invisible specter. He insisted that it was nothing more than a figment of her imagination, that would, no doubt, earn her a place in Bellevue Hospital if she continued to behave, as he put it, in the gentlest manner he could muster, "*como una loca.*"

Carlotta found Coco loitering in her clothes closet. She immediately put squares of camphor and cloves of garlic inside, much to the dismay of Che, who swore the couple would never be invited anywhere now that they smelled like a mixture of a doctor's office and a pizza parlor. Chicha saw him as she took the subway to work and missed her stop. She continued on to South Ferry, though, where the conductor had to gently pry her off the train with the assurance that she was the only one left. He finally got her out of the subway car and directed her to a taxi stand, because she refused to ride back unless she was above ground. Alberto, who had decided it was time to recapture his manhood, saw Coco sitting in a booth at Clark's Bar and left without touching the beer he had ordered. He swore that Coco sneered at him so horribly that his stomach turned and he barely made it outdoors before throwing up.

Gloria, dressing for an intimate dinner with Elliot, saw Coco in her make-up mirror while she added a touch of rouge to her cheeks. Up to that point she had been enjoying Elliot's flowers, candy and compliments. It had been years since she was told by a man how beautiful she was, but all of that seemed minor to her now, haunted by a ghost. In a panic, she canceled his visit, because if Coco could see her, then she was certain that Pedro was also watching her every move. This prompted a hasty visit to Wood-lawn Cemetery. She had not been as faithful with her trips there to replace the dead flowers with new ones as she had been in the past, while at the same time checking to see if anyone else bothered to remember her dear, deceased husband by placing flowers of their own.

Gloria threw herself back into widowhood with a passion; she convinced herself that she had not allowed the proper amount of time for mourning to pass. She no longer answered Elliot's calls and took to wearing black again. It was only after avoiding many of Elliot's advances that he showed up with Doña Josefina, who was no slouch  herself when it came to witchcraft. The old lady blew smoke around Gloria's head and commanded the dark spirits to leave the apartment. She ended her spell by pouring the entire contents of a can of Schaefer beer over Gloria's head. Gloria was shocked at first, but as she reached for paper towels to wipe up the mess, the weird old lady assured her that this was all part of the ceremony and that no spirits would make their presence known to her again.

The only person who seemed to welcome Coco's visits was Doña Esperanza. She had just finished her last session with one of the many people who came to her for advice when El Bobo began to convulse and speak in a voice that was strange to her. El Bobo began sobbing inconsolably, only to then became irrationally angry. Doña Esperanza, having dealt with many unhappy, lost and wandering spirits in her lifetime, recognized that of Coco. She consoled him and assured him that she was there to help him find the peace he was seeking. She realized that he was not there by accident and had appeared deliberately to share information with the only one who would listen to him. Doña Esperanza was eager to hear him recount the tragedy of his life with Sarah and his son—really the son of Alberto, which came as no great shock to her, having pegged Alberto as a Jekyll & Hyde shortly after his marriage to her daughter.

Although El Bobo remembered nothing of these visitations and happily greeted visits from Alberto, Amada and their two little girls, Esperanza, who never mentioned infidelity by name, made certain that Alberto understood that her innuendoes were clearly directed toward him.

Amada, ever the innocent, never understood why her mother had changed so dramatically toward Alberto, who no longer caused her distress and in fact had become a very loving husband and devoted father. One evening, while El Bobo and Alberto played checkers in the living room and Milagros was taking secret swipes at her unwanted baby sister, Esperanza decided that to impart anything other than a warning to her daughter to be careful would only end up in an argument. Amada had never taken kindly to her mother's interference, especially when it pertained to spirits and what they might have to say.

"Well I, for one, don't give any credence to these visions of Coco's ghost," declared Amada.

Doña Esperanza just shook her head and walked away. "There's no talking to you, I give up. Someday you'll find out the truth, but then again, I hope you don't find out anytime soon. I just pray God will forgive you when you do."

"God forgives everybody."

"*¡Idiota!* There's no talking to you. The conversation is over. Someday you'll see with your own eyes what you have been blind to all along."

## ∼ Thirty-five ∼

HAD DOÑA ESPERANZA been aware of the stupidity that was about to take place, perhaps she could have avoided the tragedy that would follow. She woke up that morning with a terrible migraine headache and, although Joaquín did his best to treat her pain with cold wash rags to her head, she could not get out of bed. There was no option for him but to make excuses all day long to the constant stream of visitors who left disappointed that Esperanza would not be able to transfer the many burdens from their shoulders onto her own. This headache was one of many she had suffered lately, and she should have heeded the advice she gave so many others: "Rest and take care of yourself."

"If we could just have a minute with her," they begged, while El Bobo played bouncer to the hilt. The answer was No, and that's all there was to it. He took particular joy in rebuffing Elliot's mother, whom Esperanza had immediately disliked for no other reason than she spoke of *espiritismo* all too freely without knowing what she was talking about. She had early on concluded that Josefina was a dabbler in magic, making her a menace to everyone. The spirits were not to be taken lightly, but rather treated with the utmost respect. It was for this reason that Esperanza had warned Amada not to listen to the woman, who spoke of the great powers she possessed. Esperanza knew boasting of powers was taboo; those gifts were not to be toyed with. The only great power was that of God, and Esperanza was his servant. The more she warned against this charlatan, the more inclined Amada was to defy her mother.

Amada now, as she had throughout her life, continued on the defiant path that she had chosen the day she first felt ashamed of her mother. Other parents didn't talk to spirits, making their children a mockery to the rest of the world. She resented being labeled "the witch's daughter."

Most of all she resented being second to the spiritualism which had robbed her of her mother's attention, like a child whose parent shows more care to a sibling. She was a stepchild in Esperanza's field of attention and felt very much like Milagros was feeling toward Iliana.

Elliot's mother had a mission, and little did she know that she was being used as the devil's pawn to fulfill it. Although she spoke few words, she watched everything, especially the evil presence that hovered around Amada. She could see the dark figure very clearly and was determined to be the one to rid the young girl of this evil. So one afternoon, visiting Amada, Josefina confronted the darkness, urging him to make himself known, challenging him to show himself. Finally, his presence over-powered the room through Amada. He began to moan and weep in deep guttural sounds which frightened Josefina. She quickly lost control of the encounter.

Josefina had captured his attention only to be stunned by his violence. The spirit, lost and with no answers for the woman who had taunted him, angrily shook the chair in which Amada sat, furious at having been disturbed. He had been a part of Amada's life for many years, only aware that he hated her, which he now repeated over and over again. "Why?" There were no answers. He just lashed out at Josefina's questions, threatening to kill those who dared to ask anything of him.

Amada began cursing the old woman, using words that were new to her tongue. She struck the woman with her fists and threw her aside like rubbish, all the while spinning around the room like a tornado. Summoning her weakened powers, Josefina tossed holy water and blew smoke at the spirit, who just laughed a great booming laugh that seemed to go on forever. Then, quite suddenly, the room fell into eerie silence and the spirit pretended capitulation. The darkness lifted. He seemed to be summoned elsewhere.

Satisfied she had completed her mission, Josefina gathered herself together and gave Amada a few passes with the holy water, after which she left triumphantly, boasting of her victory to Gloria, who was in total awe of the woman and her miraculous powers. Elliot was waiting in the car to drive his mother and Gloria to City Island for fish and chips, and they had left him waiting much too long as it was. Gloria and Josefina took their leave of Amada, happy that she was rid of the darkness that had plagued her. As she left the apartment Gloria thought perhaps today would be the day that Elliot would finally loosen his purse strings and pay for the meal, which in her mind would *really* be a miracle.

As the trio made its way onto Pelham Parkway, Amada cleaned up the mess that had mysteriously been created. She would never reveal what had transpired to her mother, because Doña Esperanza would chastise her for believing in the powers of anyone else. She had no idea her mother would once again be right, only this time it would not be accompanied by a smug, "I told you so."

Sarah felt the anger of the darkness storm into the tiny, furnished room that had become a temporary home for her and her son. She had been pacing the floor like a caged animal, waiting for its return. Jorge slept in his bed, unaware that his mother had poured Florida water in a circle on the floor and dropped a match, watching it burst into bright flames. Donning a red robe, she held a pair of scissors in her hand and muttered angrily, crossing back and forth through the flaming circle until it finally extinguished itself. She ran screeching across the room, calling on all of the powers of darkness, and plunged the scissors into a black, female-shaped candle that had been placed with its back to its male counterpart.

~ ~ ~

It was at that very moment that Amada heard Iliana cry out. Amada rushed into the room to find little Milagros holding a tiny pair of scissors that had been carelessly left in the sewing basket by Gloria, who had been baby-sitting while Josefina treated Amada. So as not to upset the child, Amada gingerly stepped toward her, hand outstretched, and took the scissors from Milagros. As she stepped backward a rubber toy squeaked beneath her foot, causing her to lose her balance. Amada fell to the ground and screamed as blood rushed from her eye, which had been ripped from its socket by the scissors in her own hand.

The pain tore through her like a hundred knives. She screamed again with all her might, but no sound left her body.

"I'm sorry, Mommy," Milagros said, seeing the damage she blamed herself for and not knowing what to do.

"Mommy, mommy," she repeated over and over again, but Amada gave no answer.

Antonia heard the commotion upstairs earlier during that horrible old woman's visit and now the desperate crying of her granddaughter. She searched for the spare key with trembling hands, grabbed it from its hiding place and ran upstairs. Within minutes she was calling 911.

# ～ Thirty-six ～

THE NEWS OF AMADA'S ACCIDENT spread quickly, barely giving Josefina and Elliot enough time to pack up and hightail it back to Venezuela. Realizing her mistake in overestimating her powers, Josefina knew it would not be long before Gloria opened her mouth to Doña Esperanza, who would undoubtedly go after the fool and her son with a passion. Not surprisingly, Gloria of the very big mouth said nothing. To reveal what had transpired would have made her an accomplice, and she would never have been able to face the consequences of Esperanza's wrath. As it was, she was certain the angry spirits would be looking for her, and she prayed a novena to St. Jude, begging for his intercession in what certainly qualified as a lost cause if ever there was one.

Amada also remained silent, blaming herself for what had occurred. In answer to her mother's probing, she said she had no enemies, and far be it for Alberto to suggest otherwise. In his mind he had been a faithful husband. The past had become exactly that. His harmless fling with Sarah had ended almost as quickly as it began. He had never really cared for her, and as far as he was concerned there was nothing more to their relationship than a few sexual encounters that had led nowhere. What he didn't know, of course, was that the past had never left the present and would remain entwined in his life forever.

Antonia had kept the secret of her son's illegitimate child hidden in her bosom, not even Pepitón was aware of the meeting that had taken place on the day of Coco's suicide. Antonia had convinced herself that to reveal the truth would only inflict injury on the innocents in the matter, namely her two granddaughters and their mother.

Pepitón had noticed subtle changes in his wife's demeanor, attributing it to change of life, but there was no excuse, not even menopause, for the money that was missing from the weekly receipts. His instincts were to immediately blame his son, whom he had entrusted with a key to the register. Then, one afternoon, Antonia confessed to dipping into the till.

"But why, Antonia?"

"What you don't know, can't hurt you," she said ominously.

That made the hair on Pepitón's back stand up, and he decided at that very moment that it would be in his best interest to never mention it again.

Though, for it to never cross his tongue was one thing, but for it to not cross his mind was another. At first he wondered if his wife was perhaps terminally ill and visiting a specialist on the days she would disappear for an hour or two. *It can't be that.* He realized she was as strong as an ox; it would take an illness of the greatest proportion to upend her. Charity was next on his list of possibilities, but he remembered her attitude toward the Girl Scouts, whisking them from her store with their boxes of unpurchased cookies—or the panhandlers who received nothing from her but a tongue-lashing along with advice on working for a living; all of which made charity a totally unbelievable answer. It was only when he noticed the cute little wiggle of her girdle-less behind while she carried a milk crate across the store that he succumbed to jealousy. If *he* still found her attractive, why not someone else? From that day on, he took responsibility for everything delivered to the store and gruffly snapped at any of the delivery men who so much as dared to greet his wife with their usual harmless jokes.

*What's wrong with you*, he thought, *becoming jealous in your old age? Do you really think Antonia would do anything like that? Nah! You're crazy.* But that didn't stop him from being nasty to the man who delivered the fruits and vegetables— because he found him slimy to begin with. *It better not be him,* he thought, *or I swear I'll cut my own throat.*

It was during this time, when everyone was worried about Amada, that the phone calls began. Amada had received a few hang-up calls at the hospital and assumed they were for the patient that had occupied the room before her. She had her room and phone number changed. It was authorized by her doctor, well-aware of the terrible depression she felt at the loss of her eye. He would take no chances that the trauma she endured might worsen.

When Amada was released from the hospital she began to receive the calls at her house. At first they appeared to be inno-cent wrong numbers that rang at all hours of the night, waking up Amada and the children but not the impervious Alberto, who never stirred until the morning. These wrong numbers, in which the female caller always apologized on the other end, soon were followed by rude hang-ups and ultimately turned into vicious calls where the voice would suggest that she keep her only eye on her husband, who was fooling around with other women.

The family was quick to initiate the two-ring, hang up, one-ring code, when calling Amada, but it was quickly broken by the cruel intruder. She seemed to know more about her than a stranger could possibly know. Alberto, who could barely look at his mutilated wife, denied any wrongdoing as he avoided her one violet eye that silently questioned his every word. He resented the

unspoken accusations and, in his immature fashion, reacted by
drowning his sorrows in six packs, which made him appear even
*more* guilty.

Antonia maintained her silence throughout the arguments she
heard coming from the upstairs apartment. It was only when she
found her son lying spread-eagle between the garbage cans in the
backyard, "drunk as a skunk," that she asked Pepitón to intervene, which he did willingly, throwing a bucket of ice water on
the "good-for-nothing son" he had sired.

# ～Thirty-seven ～

ALBERTO SAT SQUIRMING on the plastic-covered chair where he received the tongue-lashing he had been missing throughout his entire life. Avoiding his father's eyes, he stared at one of the decorative peacocks hanging crookedly on the wall. He thought of adjusting it but knew that even the slightest hint that he was not listening might cause Pepitón to further lose his temper. Instead he stared down at his size-seven shoes, which were scuffed and in need of a good polishing, as his father explained to him, in the harshest terms possible, his responsibilities as a man. This was accentuated with the threat of a good thrashing, which Pepitón would have relished performing at that very instant should Alberto think there was cause for laughter.

Alberto wept as he was reminded of his shortcomings, which were spelled out to him in great detail. He had never been a good son; witness the suffering he had put his mother through. He had never been a good husband, for Pepitón had ears, didn't he? He had never, it was repeated over and over again, truly been a good father, for never once had he gone out of his way to bring joy to his children's eyes. It was only when Pepitón had succeeded in erasing the crooked peacock and the scuffed shoes from Alberto's mind that he left his son alone to think about his part in the lives of those who had entrusted their love to him.

It was then that the particular corner of Alberto's mind that secretly sequestered his guilt and shielded him from any wrongdoing burst open, revealing to him every weakness that he had concealed there. He thought of Coco, the anger he felt upon hearing of his marriage to Sarah. He thought of the jealousy that had overtaken him when he learned that Coco had been able to have a son, while he had only been able to give his wife two daughters.

He thought of his last words to his beloved uncle Pedro on the night of his murder, angry and cruel, when he interrupted the argument between Pedro and Sarah at the gas station. He had quickly jumped to Sarah's defense, never questioning the reason for the argument. He let his uncle know that what he did in his life was no one's business but his own. He had left with Sarah that evening, even after listening to the evil curses she had flung at Pedro as she spat on the ground at his feet, never knowing that would be the last time he would see his uncle—his uncle who had been like a second father to him, and whom, he knew now, he had betrayed.

Most of all, he thought of his wife. She had been the target of Sarah's most venomous tirades when he refused to disavow his love for her, and now lay mutilated by a seemingly freak accident. He remembered the many black candles, which to him had seemed ridiculously innocuous, *for no human being had power over another, unless of course they were stupid enough to believe in that nonsense.* And yet, those same candles had been important enough for Coco to destroy along with his own life. The more he thought about the events that had followed his affair with Sarah, the more he became convinced that he had slept with the devil.

# ⌒ THIRTY-EIGHT ⌒

THE RIDE BACK FROM BRONXVILLE to the Bronx was one that Sarah dreaded. Her dream was to someday occupy the home in which she now worked, cleaning up after the snob who spoke to her only when she wanted something done. It was obvious to Sarah that the bitch of this particular family wore the pants, as she constantly bullied her husband into submissiveness. Sarah knew that if she played her cards right she would be successful in romancing the man. He had already shown a great deal of interest in her, watching her run through her daily chores.

Sarah kowtowed to the bitch's every whim, played the role of the timid Latina maid—which included a thicker accent when guests arrived for brunch or cocktails. It was when the husband would be banished to the outdoors for a cigarette that Sarah was there to supply him with an ashtray or a cool drink, which she knew he would appreciate, considering the fact that whenever he walked toward the bar, the wife had something else in mind for him to do. Sarah knew it was no accident that this family was childless, because everything in the dull routine of their life was planned. She could see the invisible ring in this wealthy man's nose and she was determined to be the one who would ultimately put her finger through that ring and drag him around like the lamb that he was.

As she waited for her train on the lonely Bronxville platform, she thought for a moment of her son Jorge, whom she had left alone in the apartment as she had done many times. She had warned him never to open the door to strangers; he was to remain sitting quietly on the sofa until she returned. Sarah had pressured him into obedience out of her fear that, should he ever be found there alone, he would be taken away from her and forced to live with cruel strangers who could never love him the way she did. She was content with the knowledge that she would find him smiling on the sofa when she arrived home.

At first startled by the movement in the shadows behind her, Sarah felt her heart pound as the familiar figure with the big ears and winning smile came toward her. Coyly, she turned away as he gently placed his hands on her shoulders. She knew that her calls to him would eventually pay off and he would, once again, find her irresistible. It was only when she turned toward him, searching his face with her triumphant eyes, that she became frozen with fear. There stood Coco, mutilated by his fall into the alleyway, his hands raised to strike.

## ~ THIRTY-NINE ~

SARAH AND HER LITTLE BOY JORGE, who Coco had lovingly nick-named Cucho, disappeared without a trace. At least, that's the way Antonia saw it. On the last trip she made to their ugly little walk-up apartment, carrying a money-filled blackmail envelope, Antonia was greeted by a short, obese stranger, clad only in his BVD's. He insisted she come inside to search the apartment if she didn't believe he was the sole occupant. Only after rousing the tenants in the neighboring apartments did Antonia enter, using them as guardians of her virtue. Rather than a beaming grandson, what she encountered were two dirty-mouthed parrots, one of which she would have liked to throttle for calling her "*Chula.*" Where the former occupants of the apartment had vanished to was an absolute mystery. Seemingly everyone in the building had been cursed with amnesia.

Terribly troubled by Sarah and Jorge's disappearance, Antonia showed up at Doña Esperanza's home for the first time ever and admitted the possibility of powers greater than her own. It was to this *bruja*, as she had called her many times behind her back, that she finally released the secret burden she bore. Despite her embarrassment, Antonia was determined to learn of the fate of her only grandson. She was surprised to learn that Esperanza knew of Jorge's existence all along.

"Tragedy," was all that Doña Esperanza could conjure up when she asked her guide and spirits for help in locating Sarah. "Horrible, murderous tragedy," confirmed the many stories of Sarah's demise, and yet the child's whereabouts remained a mystery.

Week after week, the two women prayed for answers, unbeknownst to Pepitón, who would have concluded that his wife had gone loony tunes had he ever learned of their secret séances. Oh, he was aware of the fact that Antonia and Esperanza were becoming what appeared to be bosom buddies. This fact alone indicated something was amiss, but his only admonition to his wife was that he would be extremely angry if he were ever to find out that she had placed a curse on him. This was always stated tongue-in-cheek, because although he never believed in curses, he thought it best not to take any chances.

Other than this new alliance, life went on its usual way, making its odd little turns here and there, sometimes for the better and sometimes not. Amada resigned herself to her one eye and was assured that the glass eye which she used as a replacement looked quite real and was barely noticeable. Gloria surprised everyone by running off to Venezuela to marry Elliot, who had declared his love by showering her with inexpensive gifts, ultimately threatening to join a monastery if she were to ignore his heart. Che and Carlotta moved back to the Bronx after Pepitón staked them the money to open a small record shop that doubled as a nail salon for Carlotta. She set up a table in the back of the shop, near the record player, becoming a deejay when necessary.

Alberto became a true father to his daughters. He would sip tea from Milagros' little plastic tea set, braiding her doll's hair. He was also teaching Iliana to catch a ball and play marbles. She had shown herself to be quite the tomboy, and that suited him just fine, despite the criticism he received from the more conventional elders of the family.

The darkness that had encompassed their lives appeared to be dissipating. But life has a way of taking unexpected turns, which ultimately lead to unexpected conclusions. It was the day of

Iliana's sixth birthday that was to become a turning point in the lives of all of those involved, minus Gloria of course, who sent a few postcards now and then, until she finally got tired of writing what Antonia called "bullshit" and was never heard from again.

Antonia had been called away from Iliana's party by none other than Father O'Connor, who had come upon what he thought might be something of great interest to her. When she arrived at the rectory, there was no doubt in her mind that the little boy who sat in the alcove of his office was Jorge. It turned out he had been placed in the Catholic Charities Foster Care System by state authorities. He had been living with several different foster parents after being found whimpering on the sofa by the landlord when he came to collect his rent.

Perhaps it was divine intervention—or quite possibly the long, dramatic confessions Antonia had made to the *padre* that led Father O'Connor to search for the child, if only to be rid of the same confession week after week, driving him to boredom. Whatever the reason, that child was whisked into Antonia's arms, never again to be left in the custody of strangers. This was done with a forceful cutting of red tape, because it would be "over her dead body" that Jorge would spend another day under the supervision of the nuns at the home. If there were papers to be drawn up and signed, she would remain there until they were drawn up and signed, "but come hell or high water, Jorge is coming home with me, thanks to God and the church."

After arguing, finger pointing, secret family conferences and an extreme amount of tears, Jorge was reunited with his family, just as Iliana remembered it. She knew by the age of six, when he entered the picture, and became her brother, that there was very little truth in what anyone in the family said, and she resigned herself to listening to their mythical pasts with a deaf ear.

# ⌒ EPILOGUE ⌒

There were many fights and many happy times to follow, especially for father and son, and the girls soon felt neglected and took to battling with their brother rather than each other. Doña Amada's bitterness at having to raise Alberto's illegitimate child overshadowed much of the happiness, but this lasted only for a short while. Eventually, she grew to love Jorge, for she loved her husband, who adored his son. She knew he was the bond that would keep them together forever.

It was not until many years later, after both of her parents had died, that Iliana's skepticism began to fade. It was after placing her own daughter in her cradle and walking to the window to shut out the draft that she found the glass marble that had protected her and her siblings for so many years, keeping its vigil as it stared out into the darkness, northward.